To Lie Within the Moment

Published by rimric press
First Edition, Hardback, Columbia SC, June 1998
Second Edition, eBook, Chicago IL, June 2008
Current Edition, Paperback & eBook, Charleston SC, June 2025

ISBN 0-9662635-4-5 | 978-0-9662635-4-1

rimric press is the imprint of rimric corporation
rimric is a trademark of rimric corporation

rimric.com

To Lie Within the Moment

a novella

m.r.m. parrott

rimric press

Contents

＊

*

la brisure

[...] The book which poured from my soul onto the pages of the very notebook I write in now was a novel; a work which had begun six years ago [...] I put everything I had into this work, while my physical existence was bolstered by bicycle racing. The product of this effort, *To Lie Within the Moment*, even for a first novel, satisfies my requirement for any work of art which I might dream of; it remains only for my readers to evaluate its communication [...]

Columbia, October 1997

a flourish

It is now, that the light has reached the idyllic point; it is 6:30 pm, and the Sun hangs at around 30 degrees in the sky, just breaking through the slight haze with an orange glow which fills the air. Out beyond the jetties, to the South, are small islands across a channel, suggested in their form through the somewhat misty wind which gently roars in my ears. [...] I am on a beach; but this is a mystical beach, where the water of my soul meets the sand of my body, and in this union, underneath the sky of my mind, the process of life unfolds before me.

The birds do beck in step beyond me, walking the lapping edge of the sea and gazing out in concert with me. There must be an aesthetic awareness for these birds; surely there is more food to be found elsewhere, but they comb the beach with an eye to the stars, and in their silence, display as profound a respect as any of us for the wondrous scene.

"I feel my version of the pattern will be as satisfying to me as those extra curls and dips which the bird just enjoyed above the waves...To me, *To Lie Within the Moment* is all about that flourish, and that union of the water, sand and sky in the soul, body and mind."

A flock of seven glide out, from one end of the surf to the other, just above the surface of the waves and follow each other's wing patterns and direction. Just when they appear to be entranced by their own conformity, the last and seventh bird breaks, curling off away from the pack in front, circling around again and again, but in its own direction, as if to construct a perfect flourish on the pattern which was set by the others.

Two days before the novel is to be delivered, I can see myself, my penchant for discrepancy, within that flourish. Just as I had wanted for much of my life, I have written books and set up business, all patterned after what the pack had set before me, but being expressed as my own design upon the raw possibilities which are extant. I feel my version of the pattern will be as satisfying to me as those extra curls and dips which the bird just enjoyed above the waves. I'm highly anxious about the future which will be mine, but as any who knows me can attest, I remain confident and bold. To me, *To Lie Within the Moment* is all about that flourish, and that union of the water, sand and sky in the soul, body and mind.

Tybee Island, May 1998

the naked eye

I can almost remember seeing this many colors in a summer sky; probably not in real life, but in a painting. It would be a Turner, or a Vermeer, or...at any rate, the range of light here is spectacular. The deep blue background for this canvas is overlaid with golden layers of clouds, all mirroring the falling Sun like a diffraction grating separating out the bold from the bland. It makes me wonder what meaning it could have toward my day; a day much like any other, but wholly unlike any recently.

A significant battle was won today, strewn on the fields of contemporary business. I booked some regional author's signings with Barnes & Noble, and found out from New York, that rimric press, along with its titles, will be listed in the national access for the B&N system. It doesn't sound like much, but believe me, for a new company to gain that kind of recognition [seems rare].

In a week or two, one could walk into a B&N

store anywhere, and ask for my novel; it likely will not be on the shelf, but it will be in the store's computer; which means that it will be taken seriously, and quickly available. This is a victory, which would not have been possible even two or three years ago. Now the other chains will be hearing from rimric press [...] The colors of this sky are as brilliant as I can imagine, and the golden light which falls upon my face must actually pale in comparison to that which emanates from my core. I feel quite alive and happy to be here, fountain before me, soaking this in. The light of this day will not soon be forgotten.

Columbia, June 1998

pivot point

"The dollars aren't coming in, just yet," he said of his life, "but they will be soon." He nodded his head at some abstract point in space just beyond me, as I sat at the table watching him. He had reached a new level in his life, he had reported, a new success for himself, and, although it wasn't currently paying off big, it was going to do so soon, he assured us both. The dollars were going to come in, and in what they provide for the spirit, they were going to set him free, not by simply making him rich, but by rewarding him for his diligence.

I believed him, as surely as I could have believed anything, sitting in Greenville last night, with a sign adjacent to me which read, "Barnes & Noble Welcomes M.R.M. Parrott author of," and in place of the title itself, they had laminated an enlarged version of the book jacket for *To Lie Within the Moment*, with the date and time below. On the table were ten or twelve copies of the novel. Occasionally someone would come pick one up, asking "what's it about," then ask me to sign it for them. Each time, a nice conversation surrounded this, and there were even several conversations which did not result in a signing, but which allowed for a mutual understanding.

This was just such a moment, and as this gentleman nodded at the world, I nodded back along with him, and became struck with the same type of feeling about my own situation. All of my hard work had brought me reeling toward this particular point, and now I could feel how its sheer importance would act as a pivot, allowing everything afterward to be seen in a new light. My writings, designs, and research has all lead me to this pivot point - my first book signing. How much better can life be, when I'm able to create the work I love to create, and, after presenting it to others, they appreciate it and reward me with complicity and grace? It only remains for the "dollars to come in," and, as I nod to the world around me, I'm sure they will come in sometime.

It is the most perfectly beautiful summer day, as the clear blue sky brings wind to my face. The colours are as vivid as any dream would have them, and I sit here writing underneath a huge Oak tree, which surely was, at one time, a lovely little acorn...

Greenville & Columbia, August 1998

To Lie
Within the Moment

a novella

*

Jim Mercer had decided he would go sailing, then. It seemed to him that, if Mary was going to be so impossible, and thus ruin the beauty of the night before as well as this morning, he would have to find some other way to enjoy the Brahms melodies in his head, for she would make sure to ruin them too, for the way things had been going lately, that was a distinct possibility. It is not as if I am running away, he thought; it is not even an argument, yet. Mary just...sits there and stares at me without saying anything, undoubtedly waiting for me to break, what must be the terrible silence, so she can pounce on anything I might dare say to her, thus interpreting my words as a threat. I simply want to go out on the bay and sail today; it is really no more complicated than that for me right now; it is not an escape, as I have tried so many times to convince her; I haven't even been out on the water in over a month. I have to get out into the air and try to think about things in my own time.

It always reminds me of the time, so many years ago, when Mother was scolding me; for spraying water on the cat while I was washing her old Daimler-Benz. It is not as if, even within such a stupid example, that I wanted Mother to shut up; to stop talking to me, it is only that I simply had to go away from the scene, to get out and far away, to go away and be limited by no one; to be with no one, and hear no voice other than my own inner one. Of course, Mary hates that I feel the need to get away, and this puts me in the most stressful type of binds, because I am certainly going to scream to high heaven if she will not leave me alone with this staring this morning!; yet I want her back. I confess it; I want her to be back in the house in Mobile; I want her to be back into my life, as well as for me to be back into hers; and I want her to get back to her paintings; while I'm wishing, I also want her to stop driving a wedge between Anna and I, to stop ruining what we all have. I just need to get out and think all of this over, just toss it around, and also let her cool down a bit, so I am going sailing.

I can't, for the life of me, figure out what she wants me to say, here; does she want me to say that I am the one to blame for what happened last night?; does she want me say that she is the one to blame? Or, on another level, am I just supposed to be the supportive one and say that I love her, and I miss her, that I can't live without her!; or should I only say goodbye, as if there is no problem, and go out sailing? I am just not able to tell what is expected of me, here, and there again, that brings me right back to the problem! Why should I be the one to play some kind of a game to get her to come back to her life? Why do I have to be the one who plays this game, only to be resolutely blamed for it later on? In all of our six years together, I have never known for things to be so complicated between us in this way; for them to be this confusing. I think I will go sailing.

Jim lay completely silent in the bed next to Mary, listening to an internal music; a collection of favorite themes from Mozart, Beethoven and Brahms symphonies and concertos, as both of them were intent only on staring at the now faintly lit ceiling, only just struck visible by the very first few moments of the morning light which came into the peach colored bedroom through the large glass doors. The both of them had said nothing to each other, not a single word since the late night before, and both had tossed and turned in their short time of sleep, each waking intermittently, only staring blankly, and saying nothing. As they both lay quiet, the subtle early morning light came into the bedroom from the sky over the Gulf of Mexico and began to delicately illuminate them, through the conduit of the window, which was framed by the size of the glass doors facing out toward the water of Perdido Bay. The faint light from the morning began to fill the warmly painted room with a cold, blue glow as they lay still, and it spilled then onto their faces, and onto their eyes, as they continued to look at the ceiling in unison and say nothing to each other.

Mary Louis-Mercer had tried to figure out how she could be so stupid. Such a ridiculous plunge into the mire!, she thought. What was I thinking? What was I doing? I would not even blame him now if he decides to go out sailing; I was such an idiot! Just like when I was in high school, she remembered, when she was seventeen, back in Point Clear. That date with Danny, she thought, Danny Boulen, the class jock. They had parked for a little while at the pier in Fairhope, and managed, to her complete amazement, to kiss for an hour in his car, then they went back to Point Clear, to her parents house, which stood on Mobile Bay. They walked down to the little building which served as a boat house and storage room, and went directly inside. They kissed and even talked, and, of course, made love on a cot which her Dad had kept from the days of mastering Boy Scouts; I wanted him so bad, she thought; but afterward we lay on the cot and I felt guilty, like I was not doing the right thing at the time. I regretted it ever after. But there!, it's a moment of truth. Is Jim like Danny for me?

Am I a great big idiot for going back with my husband after such a short separation? Well, I guess I haven't gone back yet, we only slept together after a two week separation. I just feel like I have not come to the point where I should have been, before doing what we did last night, if that makes sense. Maybe, I will let him go, let him go, without a bit of sass, out to that boat so he can sail and so I can think; I will think, think, think, and see what I should do. I will talk to Anna about it later, since I think that I am supposed to have lunch with her. Sweet Anna, she always understands, she always makes me feel so good about myself. Jim is so damned serious all the time, I can't compete with him on that level anymore; I can't lie anymore to myself about my shortcomings in his eyes.

Jim crossed his arms quietly, disrupting entirely the motionless scene which they had created, but he made no other bodily motions or sounds, but for the music in his head. Why should I just lie here and deal with all of this silence, he thought, when I have dealt with it all before? She only wants to place a guilt trip on my shoulders, or some strategy very much like that; but is it my fault, and my fault alone, that we haven't been so happy of late? Is it my singular desire to analyze everything, even my enjoyment of it, to be the sole reason for this separation? No, I think there are certainly other factors, some which she, of course, will not even listen to me explain; and so I am going sailing! Jim was not usually so huffy, especially inwardly, but he had been down this road and listened to this clever attack many times before with Mary, and he did not see the use in hearing any of it again. Mary could stand it no longer, and felt that in this very instant, she could make or break the situation into what it was going to be. She decided to go so very far out on a limb and slice through the silence with a few well chosen words; at least it was her intention that they would be well chosen.

Why are you so quiet?, Mary asked, which, unfortunately for her, also came with that tone of voice she could have, which makes it sound to Jim as if it were somehow wrong, somehow a moral failure, to be silent. Jim was thinking that it was too late, for in that short sentence, the flood gates were fully open and now they would be committed into an argument which nobody could win. Of course, her own quietude was not a valid topic of analysis during these discussions. But Mary knew she was also quiet, thinking, it is not the same kind of quiet for me. I am not 'quiet', I'm thinking; where Jim here is actively being quiet, he is being quiet as a tactic. It does seem silly, though, but what would Anna say to us? That's just it, see, she would not say anything in particular, she would just be quiet; but a good kind of quiet!; while she enjoyed the moment. I can't seem to do that; Danny Boulen would surely laugh at me now; he always said I did not seem to worry about much; could he have been right?; I guess in some ways I will never know.

Jim did not even attempt to respond to her tactical question, for he well knew that it would sink them securely into the mire immediately; he was still thinking about why he was quiet; for what is quiet?, he thought. I am at least trying to figure out what to say.

Not satisfied with the result her question had garnered, and certainly not against, in principle, the use of force in the battle to make her point, Mary turned to Jim and began kissing his cheek. She rolled her body up on top of his and kissed all over him as she tried to decide just what she was trying to do. She straddled him and continued to kiss, and made up her mind as to what direction she would steer things. Mary thought her plan was indeed cunning in its use of the feminine wile. Meanwhile, Jim, not one in a position to truly complain at this point, naturally started to be drawn into her sensuality and began to kiss her back, as he also began caressing her arms, shoulders and breasts. Mary continued to kiss her husband, but in a daring effort to maintain both her sensual mood, and her critical stance, decided to resume her speech under the guise of sexuality.

I have wanted to talk with you ever since I left you, Jim, she said; she rubbed her cheek against his after speaking in a definitely breathy voice, continuing her kissing and tonguing, massaging his face as he purred from the attention; I've wanted to talk with you even long before, she added, but...; kissing him; you are so...; continuing; you have some kind of an attitude; she moves down his neck and chest, licking his nipples; it makes me feel as if I am stupid; she looked up at him for emphasis, with her chin on his chest, speaking still in her best sexy voice; like you are looking down your nose at me intellectually, she finished. Jim kept his head relaxed, but then quickly corrected his position by attempting to sit up and place his elbows behind him for support, realizing that his body language had him looking down his nose at her.

Mary; he quipped, sitting up and caressing her cheeks with both hands, kissing her faster now.

They began to get more excited, and Jim rolled Mary off of him, onto her back on the other side of the large bed; he got up on top of her, and between her legs; he kissed her more violently on the mouth, neck and breasts as she started to purr and moan. He began to work his way downward from her neck toward her stomach, then down to her waist, then on to her groin.

I don't suppose this is the best time to talk, she said, interrupting Jim's quest; but when is it with you? You do not listen, she continued in her breathy voice; I can't get it across to you...; he then stopped and looked up at her; that I'm not happy, she finished.

Don't worry, he said seriously, I know that you are unhappy. He changed his mood abruptly, realizing that she was somehow pleading with him to be the solution to her problem, while they both knew that she was her own problem. Jim sat up, and looked at Mary with eyes which could not find her guilty of any wrong, for he well understood that she was powerless against the emotions she had been feeling. He gently touched her face with a smile, then slipped out of the silken bed, allowing only those motions necessary which would move his body, since he did not want her to think that he was angry, even though he was. His exit exposed both of their nude figures as he pushed back the camel colored sheet, showing their tan from the Gulf Coast Sun. Their bodies were fit and youthful, even though they both were no longer precisely young, Mary being twenty-eight and Jim thirty. He got up on to his feet and walked over to the double glass doors, pulled them open to the weather, since they had been shut all night, which left the room a bit stuffy. The long white curtains were filled with the cool, humid dawn air coming off of Perdido Bay, and they began to float over the floor. Jim decided that he would break his silence with a few words, hoping beyond hope itself, that they would soothe Mary and allow her to feel comfortable.

And so, Mary, he blurted, but quickly corrected; you've been gone now for two weeks, or so. You have been out here, waiting supposedly, and I've stayed away over in Mobile, waiting. I came out here last night only to break the ice; Anna had told me you were here; and, okay, so we slept together, so what, I know, maybe we should not have done that so soon, but there, we did it, it's done, and it was great, by the way. He turned toward her, standing alone in his nakedness, offering up his humility, so that she might feel more at ease. But Mary could only feel that she had made a mistake, that somehow she should have gone to Anna's, or at least somewhere other than the beach house which they had picked out together.

Oh Jim, she lamented; I feel so weak sometimes; I tried to get away from what was bothering me, and all I did was to come here, constantly reminded of you. I tried to get myself clear of you so I could think, and we wind up sleeping together. It was, for Mary, all Jim's fault, she thought, and it is just like a man, for he comes in here and thinks he can cover over everything with his sex. I have got to somehow put an end to this relationship; it is simply not as charming as it once was! But I don't know, maybe things are okay; I can't see straight right now; that is why I need time to think.

Mary thought of Anna, the friend who alone will help her, for she always has, she thought. Mary remembered the first time she had met her. It was at the art show and party she and Jim had given, Anna had been invited, since she was one of the up and coming art photographers at the time. Anna had invited Mary to visit her studio, so she obliged. They sat on the bright metal balcony which overlooked the ocean at Anna's beach house. Anna served up some tea and cake after lunch and the two of them talked about the most normal things they could think of as they sat languidly, and fully reclined. After what seemed to be too much of this good conversation, Anna asked if Mary would like to see the studio.

Of course, Mary replied.

They both stood and left the balcony, walking through the large, all white and glass living area to the hallway, their path dotted with various photographs. They made their way slowly to the dark, windowless studio and stepped into the room.

Well, here it is, Anna said, as she switched on the lamps, which threw warm yellow light across the room; she turned in place with her hands in the air; here is where I work my butt off, she added.

It's wonderful, Mary said, looking around the studio, which was cluttered with various props, lighting equipment, cameras and backdrops. This is lovely, she added, focusing on a print hanging on a nearby wall, an abstract work in black and white tones, revealing no particular object, its layers of white laying over grays, over darker grays, over blacks.

That's...well, I should let you guess, Anna said brightly, fully confident that, even though Mary liked the work, she would never guess what it represented.

I don't know what it is, Mary stumbled.

It's a flower.

Really?

Yes, it's blown up beyond belief, Anna reported, it's done with a wide lens, then...well, it's not important how the technical things come together.

Yes, I see it now. It's absolutely stunning, Anna; Mary then looked more intently at the features of Anna's face, which made her countenance happy and very childlike, for a woman of twenty-nine. Her deep brown hair was draping her neck and shoulders, and she wore a short, red wool jacket dress with matching heels. She looked back at Mary, at her blonde hair which was permed and moussed, at her navy blue pinstriped pant-suit, and at her tan face, which was excited.

Anna decided to take a chance with Mary and walked over to her; she raised her hand and stroked Mary's hair and leaned inward, placing a tender kiss directly onto Mary's lips.

I'm glad you came by today, Anna said. Mary,

though to her great surprise, was not shocked, and certainly not offended, for she found Anna seductive and beautiful. It was simply the matter that this had never come up with her before. A lesbian experience? What a discovery!, she thought. An extramarital affair with Anna Lipscomb? What a curious notion!, she noted. Mary decided in that moment of wonder to throw completely at risk her finely constructed world for just an instant; to let the walls down which had stood as strong barriers for the intrusion of the world outside; she let floods of emotion gush forth as she immediately fell into the sexual draw of Anna's eyes. Mary returned the kiss Anna had given her, putting her hand on Anna's shoulder. Perhaps, as she was wondering, this could be...; she interrupted her own thought and allowed herself to wrestle no more with worries about where this might be heading, and freely let her soul pour into the eyes in front of her.

Their kisses became more passionate as Anna began to move her hands over Mary's outfit. Then Anna unbuttoned her jacket dress, revealing her unadorned body beneath the wool. She kicked off her heels as Mary began to unbutton her pinstriped jacket, then her white blouse underneath, showing Anna her breasts. She slipped out of her pants and kicked off her heels as well. They stood facing each other with their arms around them, their breasts rubbing against each other's, kissing. Anna drifted her kisses down to Mary's breasts, then her stomach, and into her crotch, as Mary began to tingle with stimulation. Not wanting to spoil things, but also wishing to move into the bedroom, Anna gently pulled Mary away from the studio, flicking off the lights, which threw darkness over the room. They walked across the white hallway into Anna's well brightly lit bedroom...

Mary suddenly realized that she had drifted off from the scene at hand and looked back at Jim with a certain disdain for having thus ruined her memory, though he did nothing, as he looked out the glass doors at the slow revelation of the day. She pulled the sheet up to cover herself, feeling some how over-extenuated into the present space. Mary felt utterly confused as to what was going on in her head. Never before had she been so distanced from her own inner self, yet at the same time, she had never been so close.

Mary, I'm going sailing this morning, Jim reported. I think I should just leave you alone, let you think. I'll be back before lunchtime, probably around ten, we can talk then. He was standing still at the open doors, the curtains were rustling in the breeze, gently blowing against the skin of his leg.

Mary sat still in the comfort of the bed, feeling surely defeated, humiliated somehow by Jim. Why is he leaving me now, doesn't he love me anymore?, she asked herself. Every time I feel like I'm getting close to saying something profound, he goes off sailing, something like that. If I'm lucky, I can interrupt him while he's reading, so he can make me feel like I'm asking too much. He just stands there, not even looking at me, staring out and away from me, toward some far distant place I suppose, some prettier place far away from the pallid scene that he must see in front of him. Whatever! I don't care anymore what he sees within me. He thinks I've got all these problems, he thinks that I'm unstable. Whatever! I'm not unstable! I'm just...I'm just a pathetic idiot! What was I thinking, letting him come back inside me again, letting him...what was I thinking? What was I thinking? I must be pretty stupid. I should have just stuck with Anna; I should have left Jim completely and stayed with Anna until I could figure something out. But no, he had to come here and visit, he had to come here and be nice to me, he had to tell me he loved me.

But maybe he does? Maybe he does love me and I am just a dried up piece of shit; my work has suffered, I can't seen to paint like I should; hell, it hasn't just suffered, it has been nonexistent. I can't work like Anna does; it's seems so easy for her to come up with these great prints; I can't get ideas like Jim does, it's seems so easy for him too! Why do I suffer like this! Why can't things be as easy for me as for them! Why do I have to feel the sting of my mediocrity at every turn, waiting for me to give in, to collapse into a puddle of tears, so I can give my art over to the modern machine! And so he stands there, with his incredible audacity to be happy, only looking off in the distance, toward the sunrise with a gleam in his eye; he doesn't know the pain I suffer. Woe, then, to the settled thinker, all alone in his padded room.

Jim turned from the now glowing light of sunrise to look at Mary. She seemed to him to be so unhappy and volatile, and he knew how lost she must feel, but he knew, for fear of falling into a demonic tennis match, not to even think about pushing to hard; for in the five years of previously blissful marriage he had at least learned one thing that sets her off every time; Mary does not tolerate even the hint of pushy behavior, but, of course, these days, and especially this morning, it was so very difficult to figure out any behavior that she would tolerate and not perceive as a threat. He had to keep trying, of course, for he wanted her to feel comfort, rather than pain; for his part, in order to do this, he had to remain affirmative in the face of such a 'negational' pain, for what else could he possibly do, he repeatedly asked himself, over the last few months.

I love you Mary, Jim said, trying to give her everything that she could have wanted from him emotionally. If you want me to go back to the main house today, I will; I'll do anything you wish; but I really want to go out and sail today. It will give us a chance to maybe think things through a little more; I'm really so sorry you are upset at me; at least you seem to be upset. Perhaps we did too much too fast, but if you want to talk...I can...

Go, go!, she said with command. Go ahead and sail, Jim, don't worry. I'm okay with it. I want you to go...you're not bound to stay here...

Well, don't make it sound like I'm trying to get away...

Just go, Jim!

They both froze in place as the tension rose quickly, in the dimly lit room. Neither of them had ever raised their voice to the other, for any reason, and now Mary had ruined that. For Jim, she had shattered the relationship in one fell swoop, in that one slip of the tongue. Mary opened her mouth to say something, but quickly silenced herself, realizing that there was nothing she could ever say to apologize for screaming at Jim in anger. Sorely defeated, is how she now felt.

Defeated, once again, I am a defeated fool, thinking to herself. She raised her hand up to her forehead and scratched an itch, while staring at the mussed sheets of the bed. What a fool I am. We indeed had a passionate night, and because of that he expected me to come back. Of course! My Jim was only trying to ride it out so I would come back and be happy; he was only trying to help, and it would have worked, until I screwed it up! Defeat has a sting like nothing else I know, she laughed to herself. My veins are thumping against my skeleton with each painful heartbeat. The blood seems to boil my brain as my ears ring loudly, and I feel only a deep self hatred. It is a hatred so loud that it drowns out all other feeling I am capable of, making my body hum with a distinctly red vision. Damn it! What is going wrong? Did I do wrong by sleeping with Jim last night? Perhaps, I should not have left Jim to begin with? Is it really the end of our marriage, or am I only a stuttered and confused psycho?

The tension was now falling within Jim, for he only looked at Mary with an inquisitive glance; how much I do not know her, he thought, how much I wish I could reach out to her, but, as she continues to push me away, I realize that my help is no good; she must learn to help herself. Who is this woman in front of me?; this woman I have called the love of my life?; what has gone on within her spirit to pull her so far away from the unity of her own identity? Ironically, she is, in this moment, the stark opposite of anyone I would want in my life, but I have to think of this as only an instant in our relationship. Soon, things will be different; there will come another moment to follow this one; I will once again return to loving Mary, because she will either return to her old personality, or she will invent a new one which I will be delighted to meet. Like Alice in her wonderland, we will get somewhere, if we just walk long enough.

I'm sorry Mary, he said, still trying to give her as much as she could have needed emotionally, let's talk later, I'll just be out in the bay. Jim moved away from the open doors, gathering his clothes from the floor, and then went into the dark green hallway, feeling defeated. Mary dropped her hand to her lap and looked outside blankly; a tear began to well up in her eye and rolled down her cheek, for she felt that she had ruined everything. Jim paused for a moment in the hallway, at the cream colored staircase banister, and found himself looking at the black and white print he had made four years ago, a photograph of Mary in bust profile, standing on the beach. Jim let himself fall into the soft contrast of the bright photograph, noting the scale of white, gray and black; he easily remembered how things were that day at Pensacola Beach.

...I would do anything for you right now!, Mary had called to Jim, with her hair flying in the wind in a relaxed curl; her long, peach linen dress was hugging her figure; her bare toes were buried in the white sand.

Would you now?, he returned, as he was approaching her from twenty yards off, barefoot as well; the cuffs of his blue slacks were still wet from his jaunt in the surf. He unbuttoned his blue striped, white pinpoint and let the tails fly free in the wind as he heard an old Duran Duran tune in his head.

Yes! What is it that would you have me do?, Mary said with a huge grin as Jim drew nearer to her; then Jim held his camera up to his face, pointing it at Mary.

Put that down, she said, I'm not dressed for pictures! Jim! What would you have me do? Jim got closer to Mary as she smiled.

Would you marry me? Jim then quickly shot a frame of Mary as she reacted to his question.

What? Mary was smiling; but Jim, dear, she added, we are already married!

No we're not!, he said playfully.

Yes we are, you goober; here, do you see this ring? Mary put her hand, which sported the plain gold wedding band, right into his face for emphasis.

Yes.

How do you think I got this ring?

Your last boyfriend, I guess!

You are cracked!, she said as she pushed him away with both hands.

But I love you, he said, directly.

I love you more, she reported.

Then marry me, again?, Jim asked, and they both stood glimmering into each other's eyes.

Yes, she said, without questioning her thoughts.

What a tender scene, Jim said, sarcastically, and kissing Mary. She smiled at him and looked out at the Gulf of Mexico. Jim stepped back and took another frame of her as she beamed; he took another and another as he watched her take in the beauty of the day before her...

I miss that Mary, he thought. She was in many ways stoic, but deeply passionate. It is hard for me now; I can't help but see her blonde hair, flying in the sea breeze, and her distant gaze, with wide open eyes, as a chilling pretense to this far off moment of self-doubt she seems to be buried within right now. I don't know these days whether to reach out to her, or leave her alone completely. I'll have to talk with her later.

Jim stepped down the stairs, feeling a bit sad now, and upon reaching the foyer, put his khaki pants on and slipped into his dark blue shirt. He walked back to the copper decorated kitchen and began to fuss about for something to eat, but thought that Mary would not want him stumbling around in the kitchen right now. The boat is fairly well stocked, he thought. I could just run out into the big part of the bay and make up some breakfast, then loop back down and tack out toward the jetties, or whatever, I should just get going.

He walked into the dark paneled den and paused to pick up his navy blazer and brown loafers, noticing in the dim light the black stockings and high stiletto heels Mary had left on the sofa the night before during their playfulness. He stepped into his shoes and headed around through the white parlor, noting, across the foyer, in the red and brown dining room, the nearly empty bottle of Bordeaux and the glasses on the table, with their dry red film of wine. Jim pushed on toward the front door, with a tug on the latch, opening the door, which poured light onto the dim camel walls of the foyer and allowed him to notice for an instant the newer portrait on the near wall of he and Mary laughing, taken by Anna.

Jim stepped out into the welcoming morning air and light, turning away from what was a painful memory, and, sliding into the sleeves of his blazer, he took care to button his shirt and tuck in the tail. He walked over past Mary's silver-grey Mercedes sedan to his new, black convertible Jaguar, he opened the passenger door, and got a pack of cigarettes out of the glove box; though Jim had rarely allowed himself to smoke at all, he thought this to be one of those few times when it just felt like the right thing to do to match the, somehow dark, mood. He lit his cigarette and took one glance at the gray tones of the exterior of the beach residence before turning toward the gray painted, large wooden boat house on the left. It sat only about thirty-five yards away from the edge of the house, and inside, there was a boat bay for the storage of a small power boat, but Jim did not keep one. The blue-water racing boat, *Ideal*, he had owned for years, was far too large, at forty-five feet, and drew to much water, to place inside the boat house, so Jim kept it moored to a long wooden dock which stretched about ten yards toward the short beach; itself only a point on the jagged shoreline at Orange Beach. Jim went into the boat house, only to get the hidden spare keys to the companionway and motor, for he remembered that he had left the other set in the kitchen drawer over in Mobile, since he had not been out on the water in such a long time. Jim had kept in the boat house extra lines, spare rigging, light-weight racing sails, and various tools, all perfect for those frequent and lazy Saturday afternoons he had enjoyed a couple of years ago; but Jim knew the boat was currently in very good shape, so he knew that he only needed his keys. Jim thought about how he had not even envisioned being here this morning, or that he would want to go for a sail. He grabbed the keys, which were hanging on a rusty nail in the corner, though well hidden, and then headed back outside, pausing only to look up at the now bright sky of morning.

Mary sat very still in the bed. She focused her finely tuned eyes onto the sheet which hung over her knees; the now warm morning light came in through the balcony doors and poured its bath of light over the ivory white and camel bedding, creating in its path miniature ranges of mountains and other topologies across the silken sheet. Mary ran her eyes over the folds, all over the creases and the ripples; she saw the highlighted areas reflecting the morning light, and the shaded areas, only faintly lit, by the bounce of these highlights. She focused at a still finer level, revealing the minute detail of the woven threads which made up the sheet. Each thread traced a path, weaving over another thread, then under the next, on and on to describe a circuit across the valley of a shaded area then up over the crest of a highlight. No thread drew exactly the same line, as they ran in parallel and perpendicular vectors all over the fabric, over the topology of the sheet, over the expanse of the bed. A grid was formed which folded space around it and made a geometrical pattern over that space. This grid is a great canvas for three-dimensionality, she thought, as her imagination ran across one vector after another, each leading to a different point on the matrix.

Her eyes moved to the wall ahead of her. Its flat surface, spread with peach pastel paint, gave way to a more subtle dimension. It is riddled with very small undulations, she thought, yet does not benefit from the easy vectors of the grid of threads. It allows an much more detailed divisibility and directionality; offering no map, either, for the plumbing of its possible pathways.

Mary shook her head and rubbed her eyes, feeling a slight headache approaching. She then looked around the room without an agenda, blankly focusing on the caramel credenza and the side table, the portrait of her on the side table made a year ago by Anna, the camel wicker chair and the balcony doors, which were now open and pouring in the morning air and light. The balcony drew her, and she climbed out of bed to walk out onto the concrete slab, finally settling onto the gray metal rail. The wind brushed her face, and it curled around her cheeks to tickle her ears, then flew through her blonde hair to fly off of the ends. The light had covered the night over, becoming more and more yellow as the Sun rose higher, and it lit her nude, statuesque figure gracefully while she stood. Mary surveyed the blue water of the bay, the green leaves of the trees and the various colors of the October sky.

What serenity the world had for me, back then, she reminisced, for when I had finished my first canvas and stepped out onto the back lawn at Point Clear, I felt a supreme joy; what an accomplishment, for a budding artist of fifteen.

...She had rendered a scene of a classical female statue in an English garden, dotted with explosions of colors, using an artistic sensibility many artists only achieve much later in their careers. The crisp and cool January air felt good to Mary with the afternoon Sun streaming in as she walked down to the shore of Mobile Bay.

Incredible, Mary!, she heard her father shout from the patio. Mary turned away from the bay as he rushed over toward her.

Dad?, she said, not quite knowing then what he was talking about.

Mary, I just saw that painting you did. His eyes were bright and his teeth were visible.

What do you think of it?, she asked.

I think it's terrific, sweetie, that's what I think! Mary smiled, fully blushing with the flower of her youth, and certainly made very happy by her father's reaction to her achievement.

I'm glad you like it, she said, smiling...

But why don't I ever feel like that anymore?, Mary thought, turning her back to the morning wind, leaning onto the balcony's rail. She shook her thoughts away and suddenly walked away from the balcony and back into the bedroom, past the bed and into the light blue bathroom; she turned on the faucet and scooped up some water with both hands, submerging her face into it. She picked up a towel and dried her face with it, but then was caught by her own gaze in the mirror. She put the towel down onto the counter as her eyes pierced the imaginary plane of focus in the reflection and thereby trapped her within their power, duly locking her into their double stare; the reflection stared Mary down, and Mary stared the reflection down; this double reflection thus allowed no escape from the tyranny of the eyes before her. But the eyes were indeed surrounded by many other facial clues to the puzzle of Mary's strange moods. She examined her eyelids, lashes, brows, her forehead, her nose and cheeks, her mouth and chin. She pulled her mussed hair back with one hand into a ponytail and continued to look at herself; her face had therefore held the effects of her life; the slight effect of wrinkles forming, allowing the supple nature of her youthful skin to gradually diminish, becoming ever drier and less pliable, as the stress of growing past youth became apparent.

Her eyes returned to the eyes of the reflection, to the double of her which was not her; she looked at herself reflected in her own eyes and began to wonder; what was it, she thought, that happened to me, why did I fall from grace the grace of my youth? Why has the youth gone from my face? What a lovely quality it had. It was such a strange feeling to put on makeup, she remembered, for a young girl of twelve, as she was, suddenly in that moment; what a sensation! It feels like a mask, but what does this mask hide, she asked her older self; is this a veil which presents one for the perusal of an outward world?

What does the mask hide?, she asked the reflection. But it says nothing, she thought, why does it not know? Mary burst completely into tears in front of herself; she let her hand which had been holding her hair fall to the counter and she then curled over and put her head down as she wept; she was now missing her youthful face, a face so young that, at the time, she could enjoy the luxury of considering makeup only a silly mask, only a meaningless activity that girls do. There, of course, was no disturbed self-consciousness for such a youth, where now, for Mary, there is always a mask which hides something. So Mary wept, she cried and cried as she stood before the double of herself in the reflection, as she stood before the mirror of her mixed emotions.

At the end of the dock, *Ideal* seemed lonely to Jim, with its bow rising and falling with the small waves which struck it, with the wind dragging on its rigging, and causing a few trim lines to vibrate and slap against the mast. He hadn't been on the boat in over a month and was, obviously, quite excited to go out. What a vessel, he thought, I am so happy to have had this rig over the years; every one should be brought up sailing; it's good for the soul. Jim boarded the boat, tossing his cigarette butt out into the starboard water. He leapt into the cockpit and took off his blazer; he laid it over the rail and set his eyes out to the bay while he fumbled for the keys, then he unlocked and opened the companionway. He stepped down near the chart table, turned on the depth sounder, compass, and radio. Climbing back on deck he keyed on the diesel, threw off shore power, and uncleated the mooring lines, throwing them onto the dock, which allowed the boat to drift back. He sat down into the cockpit and manned the diesel, steering *Ideal* off of the wind, to head up into the bay. As he let the engine run, he unfurled the headsail, which was kept on a roller, as he steered into the wind. Then he could set the auto-helm, pull off the main sail's cover and hoist it. Now I can sail, he thought, now I can fly free, as he turned off the diesel after a few minutes.

The wind was blowing at about 15 knots that day, and since Jim liked to hoist full sail, this heeled *Ideal* far over. He sat on the weather rail, fully enjoying the boat, fully loving life, as he held the large wheel with his left hand, and kept the other resting on the safe line; he was sitting in the catbird seat, he thought, where there is nothing finer in life, than to have the wind on his face. It is only now that I feel fully actualized, that I am truly experiencing the *real* world; a world where there are no voices screaming or bodies of language. There is only the air, the water, and the incredible machine of the sail boat, a silent wonder, a craft which reels from the natural play of the forces upon it. What else could it mean to be a subject within the world, for what is subjectivity, but a product of this controlled, but empirical, passage through force, which is a projection of matter and time. Isn't that what Berkeley, Kant and Nietzsche were thinking? The play of forces are being taken up empirically by the mind and expressed as a perceptual world; this is what allows one, through living through these forces, to create an affirmative passion.

The negation within Mary began to stream out, from its deep core of her identity, to the outer reaches of her troubled consciousness; like so many satellites, her memories of childhood, her moods and her desires spread themselves out and flew their wings in an explosion of color, sound, and feeling. The center point of subconsciousness which made up her identity was slowly disintegrating as the passions she had been experiencing were slowly drawn out and dissipated. The face within the mirror was now only blank, and its energy had been drained, thereby left without a grounding. Mary stared herself down and began to grin at the reflection, but the face in the mirror grinned back with a wider mouth; she started to laugh at the reflection, but the face laughed louder and more forcefully. Mary laughed at her reflection which laughed harder and louder back at her, and with a new maniacal quality; she laughed and laughed, but then, suddenly, did not find anything funny, not in the least, and therefore stopped laughing, then checked her face in the mirror and turned away, walking into the bedroom, then into the hallway and onto the landing of the stairs, catching sight of the black and white photograph of her which Jim had taken.

You're gone, she said, pointing to her image on the print; you get it?, you're gone, and I don't like who's here. 'And I a maid at your window...,' she sang; oh, I can't seem to remember the rest of Ophelia's words, she lamented, now leaning onto the print, and onto the wall behind it, looking away with no expression.

Where have I gone?, she asked herself, where is my passion now?; what is it I have done to skew things such? She started down the steps, humming aloud pieces from several songs and reached the bottom, in the foyer. She looked over from the steps into the dark red tones of the dining room, noticing the wine bottle and glasses, then turned around and walked to the wet bar between the dining room and the kitchen. She opened a lower cabinet door, then pulled out a bottle of whiskey, taking a shot right out of the bottle, then put it back and shut the cabinet door. Mary then walked through the den to the large, sliding glass door, opened it, and went outside, not concerned at all for being unclothed, and made her way toward the sandy beach on the point, toward the bayshore.

Look at this!, she thought, what a beautiful day it is!, for such a young girl to have finished an artwork. I'm so glad to have completed my first canvas! I hope Dad likes it. But it is blank! That huge thing has no paint on it, don't you see? No, that is my last canvas, don't you know? Unfinished? No, it is not even begun! Imagine that, the last work of Mary Louis-Mercer, not even begun! Mary then ran into the lapping water of the bay, kicking her feet out, splashing up water into the air. Out on the horizon of the bay she could see the white sails of a boat, but looked away and continued to kick at the water, not even seeing it as Jim's boat in her present mood, though she knew it well, having crewed on all of the regattas.

By now *Ideal* had made out it to the middle of the 'big bay', as Jim called it. Perdido Bay was just big enough, so that if one needed to nap, or cook, or lie in the Sun, one could let the boat drift on the lines for a little while; but Jim noticed well that the wind was up today, so he knew he would have to watch things closely. Jim furled the sails and dropped the anchor, thinking about making breakfast and perhaps laying out on the foredeck for a few minutes, so he went below to make something to eat. I haven't had so much as a glass of water this morning, he realized, having been up for some two hours. He searched around in the galley fridge and cabinets for something good. There was an inexpensive bottle of wine, an unopened carton of egg whites, some pasta, some canned chicken, and brown bananas. It's time to fire the maid, he thought to himself, even knowing full well, of course, that the dear maid who kept the house in Mobile would not come all the way out to Orange Beach and stock the boat for 'all the tea in China', as he remembered she would say, with a smile on her face.

There was at least some coffee, he consoled himself, and also some vanilla flavored cream and bottled water. So, Jim set out to light the gimballed stove, and poured out some water into a pot, setting it to boil. He set up his over-the-cup coffee dripper with a filter and some grinds. Jim then pulled out the pasta and the egg whites, and threw the frozen bananas out into the bay. He poured himself a glass of water while the pot was boiling up, gulping it down without pause. The pasta was stirred in and allowed to boil after he had drained off enough of the water into the dripper to make coffee.

As the coffee dripped and the pasta boiled, Jim remembered Mary as she was sitting on the bed; her face was somehow, in the midst of the tangle of words, angelic, her blonde hair playful, her blue eyes deep and her body young and vibrant. He remembered her saying how she was restless after college, and eager to get busy on her own style of art so many years ago, how she was so glad to have met an artistic and understanding person like Jim; his creative spark was an ignition of energy for her.

...You are a very interesting person, Mary had

said, while she was leaning on the rail of an old dock on Mobile Bay; you've got a very special quality about you, I just know you'll go far in the world. I'm glad to know you, I guess I should get your autograph now, before you become famous. She laughed nervously as she fought the quiver of her lip for a brief moment in the setting sunlight.

Well, you're going to give me a big head; I'm glad to have met you too, Mary Louis, he said with dignity, bowing over and offering his hand; you know, you have the names of two saints...

Only one is a town...

Yeah. He paused and stared deep into her blue eyes, pleased that she had caught on to his sense of humor; he thought about how attracted he was to this twenty-two year old artist. She returned the gaze, thinking about how this strange philosopher had made everything seem so genuine, as if nothing was real until it was pondered deeply.

May I kiss you, Mary?

You don't have to ask me that, she quipped, blushing, as if she were a school girl presented with her very first kiss.

Jim leaned in slowly, taking in the scent of white musk on the nape of Mary's neck, fondling a lock of her blonde hair, touching his cheek to hers with the gentlest brush of the fine tiny hairs underneath her ear lobe. Their lips met for a moment, sending their heartbeats higher, then again for a moment longer, then...

Damn! Jim lamented as the excess coffee ran onto the counter, for he had poured too much into the dripper and it ran over the edge of the cup. He grabbed a towel and wiped it up, then drained a little off the top of the cup, leaving room for the cream he put in. He poured the water off of the pasta and stirred in some basil, pepper and grated cheese, then quickly remembered that the egg whites needed to be prepared, so he covered the pasta and pulled out a skillet, turning the flame back on. The egg whites were stirred in with some spices added, as well as the canned chicken, when once cooked up, Jim added them to the pasta, throwing in a little more garlic, for good measure as he gulped his coffee down. Jim then popped the cork on the bottle of wine, poured a tall glass and set out to the deck to enjoy his strange creation.

Sitting down onto the foredeck, leaning back on the cabin rake, Jim let his eyes fall out of focus as he ate. This breakfast actually tastes good, he thought, and the day is of course beautiful; I suppose things could always be worse. he thought, savoring his pasta mixture along with his wine, and as he twirled his fork around the spoon, pulling up noodles and spices with bits of protein, he took in the scene around him, noting the fully actualized nature of the day, as a culmination of a process by which a day becomes what it is going to be. Jim thought that the process of today was nearly finished with its gradual revelation, and that from here he would be actualized along with it, to complete the creation of the last remaining layers of revelation.

As he was finishing up his pasta, sipping on his wine, there was a jet plane gliding high across the blue firmament; it drew a white line across the sky as the condensation from the engines created a divider, to

Jim's mind, between one space and another; it marks out a space itself, he thought, as it divides. Could it be that this distinct demarcation divides one *moral* space from another, in a process of defining two moralities? How is it that one is to choose between them? There is no difference in them, he noted; there is only one space and another, separated by a sharp white line; but wait, this line is now fading, as the condensation goes away, it is slowly disintegrating, no longer marking either of the spaces, but disappearing altogether as a division. It becomes very hard now to say where one space ends and another begins, for there is a definite blurring of the two; where does one find respite, when there is no fundamental schism?

Jim put his now empty plate down on the deck, thinking he might take a nap, but something was nagging him, coercing him into alertness. It was guilt over Mary; I cannot leave her back there sulking, he thought. I must go on back to the house and see if I can somehow work it out with her. Jim grabbed his things, skipped down the deck and down the companionway, then cleaned the dishes and other items, and put everything away. He went back out on deck and pulled up the anchor, then set sail back to see Mary.

But the water was surely not enough to kick at for Mary; she could kick and kick, lashing out at all of the water she wanted to run to, but it would only represent a small amount of what she wanted to kick. If, thinking to herself, she could be bellicose toward the entire bay, the entire Gulf even, she would not have issued the full brunt of her dissent. Her disgust with herself was now infinite, and, as she thought, I disgust myself even more by thinking about it. I hate myself just enough to utter it, but somehow not enough, not as much as I need, to put an end to this hatred. But there it is!, she mused, lurking in all of those subterranean passages of my thought; it is the end that I wish for. The End. But the end of what? Why, the only end I can fathom, stupid, the only end for which I could live, it is the end to this hatred, to what it has produced in myself, and to what it has been doing to Jim and Anna; it is an end to the pain. This is the only end I could wish for now, it is the end me as I now know myself to be, as I am.

But why does this world press down upon me?, she called out to the sky above. It seemed to her that now the sky, the very firmament of the heavens was pushing its entire weight down upon her body and soul, pressing its depth toward her very center. The sky, the trees, the water, and earth itself were now closing in on Mary's identity, squeezing her from all directions. It became hotter and more humid for her, and her eyes began to water, sweat started to bead all over her nude body. The Sun beat her; it beat down upon her at a hundred times its normal size; now a thousand times its size; it was only yards, only inches, away from her burning and melting body, and she knelt down in the boiling water, hiding from its infinite heat and bright, white blinding light. Mary could now only see white, in all directions, and felt an infinite number of eyes upon her. The Sun, which was one large eye, became all the eyes of all the people in her life. They looked at her and began to move like mouths, singing at her in a demonic chorus.

Mary got up to her feet and ran, frightened by the panopticism of the Sun, which saw her thoughts, her moods and her very identity, holding it within a judgment, and the voices of the eyes, which pierced her ears and rang into her brain. She ran and ran, seeing only white, but managed to see the outline of a building, and she made it to the door of the boat house; she went inside, leaving the door open, but felt the eyes of the Sun leaving her alone for the moment, yet they were not far off as they beat on the walls of the building. The heat from the Sun bore down upon the roof and walls of the building, making it seem like an oven, one which cooked Mary inside its borders. Her thoughts were reeling out of her control as she recalled past scenes and sights from her life with a speed she had never known; they were fleeting images of a Mother she had barely a chance to know, who was killed when she was young; a father who supported her talent, but who went insane in later life; siblings to whom she had never felt very close; friends who never understood her deepest feelings; Anna and Jim, who became hurt, even destroyed, by her loss of passion. Images, all merely images, she thought, they are all merely haunting me, but all of them are pressuring me; their eyes shine toward me as a part of the Sun; their ascending voices are all conjoining into one powerful tenor, which is getting ever louder and louder, as they scream at me their demands.

Mary looked around the room, among the sails, lines, tools and other things stored here. She grabbed a waste-high stool from the workbench and placed it over by the boat slip, then sat down on it, hearing only the powerful voices which sung to her, seeing only the eyes which looked at her. She stood and took up a line which hung out on a wall mounted hook, and climbed up onto the stool; she had to reach in order to throw the line over a wooden rafter tie above; then she fashioned a simple loop around it, to anchor it to the rafter tie; she then made another loop at shoulder height and placed it over her head and around her neck. Trying to keep her balance on the stool, she thought for a moment about Jim and Anna, about her family, friends and acquaintances, and in thinking about them, she felt that they would be better off now. They do not deserve to be treated as I have treated them. It is their eyes and voices which have pushed me here to this point, I am fulfilling their wishes! They should all be so happy now! She looked at the wedding band on her sweaty left hand and took it off. She thought that now the ring should be placed into the ocean, the gulf, which stood between her and the others, and with that, she turned and threw the ring into the boiling water of the boat bay as the voices screamed louder and the eyes became hotter, allowing her to see only white again as sweat dripped off of her body. She turned back away from the water.

Goodbye, Jim, she said, as the tears streamed down her face. Mary then let herself fall off of the wooden stool, forcing it to fall over onto its side as her body dropped in the air, quickly taking up the slack in the line. The loop tightened around her neck and immediately crushed her larynx as her weight came to force against the resistance of the taut line. Mary's weight hung freely now by the rope she had designed and it choked her fast toward death as she looked out through her teary eyes to the door of the boat house, seeing only the light from the multitude of malicious eyes which made up the Sun, as the voices screamed louder and louder in their culminating horror. The sound of the voices and the light of the eyes slowly faded away for Mary. She was now unconscious and headed straight for her death as her body became still. The noises faded into silence and the light dissolved to black as her brain died, leaving her completely without thought. The wedding band had twirled and turned in the water, then came to rest on the sandy bottom of the boat bay. Mary's eyes stayed open as her lungs stiffened and her heart beat one last time. Her body hung dead in the silence of the building as the cool breeze came in through the open door. Outside, the wind blew across the surface of the bay and the clouds above drifted across the sky.

As *Ideal* sliced the water, lulled by the strong and variable winds, Jim imagined what he could possibly say, or what he could possibly think, to get Mary to feel comfortable with the world, and to get her to feel good about herself again. We'll take it a day at a time, and I will not try to hard to talk it all out, he thought; we'll eventually get back together in Mobile and things will be different. They have to be. I'll spend more time with her; I will do anything to make her happy and show her my love. Maybe our friends have driven us apart, maybe even Anna, a mutual and dear friend; maybe she has been like a wedge, of course, not intentionally, but quite innocently, and has created a line between us. We could to for a vacation, we could go to New York, or Los Angeles, Mary loves those places, and get away from our friends for a while, even Anna, and see some different scenery for a change.

Jim steered the boat up to dock, after furling and dropping the sails, stopped the engine, jumped onto the dock, and moored to the docking cleats. Back on deck, he plugged in shore power, grabbed his blazer, turned off instruments, secured the companionway, then leapt back onto the dock. I feel fine, he thought, like I have reached some kind of plateau, and I know now that things will be okay. I want to go back inside and tell Mary how much I love her; I want to hold her tightly in my arms tell her how much I desperately need her, and I will assure her I will be right here for her, always.

Then, with one last look toward the gentle lapping of the waves upon the sandy shore, Jim let out a sigh of relief and therefore resigned himself to having had a rather nice morning out on the bay, despite the unfortunate argument with Mary earlier; though his small passion for sunning himself was not nearly appeased today, but he thought that was no matter. He stepped off of the dock and up to the door of the boat house, pausing to look back one more time at the serenity of *Ideal*, the motion of the water and the depth of the sky. Jim opened the door of the boat house and walked in, still with his eyes on the horizon.

Turning his eyes into the boat house, a vision caught him; Holy Hell, he thought, fully stunned; what in the world is this?; my wife!, he thought, but, no!, it cannot be her! This was a sight out of a horror novel for Jim, this was not something which was a part of reality. Uncontrollably, for he had found that his entire universe had been shattered, Jim gasped and turned his back toward Mary, turning back again toward the door, leaning on its frame with his hand resting on its knob. Jim continued thinking; that cannot be my wife Mary!, it is not her!, not her!...I can't even think about it, but why...why! I must look at this apparition again, perhaps it is some type of mirage...maybe...What brought this on, he thought as he looked again at the dead body in front of him, what brought on this violent, and yet fully still assertion of pain?; what brought her to do this, I mean to take matters all the way to this level, to stand there on that stool in the final moment and proclaim, once and for all, this is it, world! By all means let's leave it all out in the open, dangling in the boat house, for everyone to see, or at least for me to see; let us be withdrawn from all melodrama, and present a finality which is to be separated from finality itself, by all means! Mary, what kind of sick and depraved animal in nature would bring matters to this fruition after such a peaceful life?; after suffering no apparent stormy outbursts, after living such a tranquil summer of a life? Why have I been made to examine the death of this flower, whose inner meaning was evidently only sheltered from the reach of my sense? This lady, who is frozen still, protects in her dead heart such a lamentable secret, buried deep within her bosom, indeed, it is buried infinitely deep.

Jim turned back to the open door as he wrestled

with the vision of Mary, then stepped outside and looked out at the beach, at the sky and water, shocked to the very core of his being. What deeds have I done, he asked himself; what plots have I laid, to set into motion such a solemn enactment of a despair which only serves to produce in her a stillness? Jim stumbled slowly out onto the sand and made his way to the shore of the bay, as his thoughts drifted out, down the length of the short beach he walked, as he thought endlessly of Mary's smile, of her supposed joy, of her artistic passion; he thought about how all of this was now trampled, all of it was silenced by this horrific event. Jim stepped very tentatively back and forth across the shoreline, thinking about Mary as she had been to him, the only way in which he could be capable of thinking about her. While the wind gently came off of the bay and pushed the door of the boat house, slowly drawing it closed, then lulling it open again, Jim was allowed an alternating view and closure, a window onto the state of his Mary, as she now was.

Jim walked across the shore once again and fell onto his knees in the hot sand, he put his head down into the open palms of his hands and wept as he became ever more disturbed by Mary's death. Never again will Mary utter my name, he thought, touch my face or hold my hand. Her blank stares, which he remembered as having given him so much toil, would now be welcome, where now, there is only a further obfuscated type of stare, one sublimated to a darker, quieter region, where even the mere possibility of an emotional purchase was abruptly silenced, thereby strangled by the overcoming black clouds. My zest for living has now been met by its inverse, its immortal opposite, whose power could only be measured with the silence it produced. Where is my sweet Mary now?!, he cried out to the sky, while looking out across the chopping water in the bay. Has her soul found its proposed peace and respite from whatever was bearing down upon her? Was this escape from living so promising in its joy that it reflected a life of such misery before its meeting! Was this dull, grey boat house on Orange Beach to be such a meaningful place in which to rest the body, to put an end to the soul?

I cannot look upon this vision any longer, he thought, as he nevertheless turned away from the bay and stood looking at the boat house, which was put into motion by its swinging door. Turning toward the beach house, Jim's soul seemed to him to lift itself out of his body; it floated well above him and looked back down upon him from the outside. The scene of Mary hanging within the boat house vanished now before him; it was for him the hottest day of September, not long ago, he thought, it was when Mary had left me, when she had moved out of the Mobile house, and disappeared from the life we had there, only to resurface days later at the house in Orange Beach, so I heard from Anna.

...It is very hot today, he thought, as he sped across the causeway over Mobile Bay, only just coming from a lunch with his Mother in Fairhope. Jim was just about to enter the old Bankhead Tunnel when, as it must have been some kind of psychic premonition for him, a window onto the immediate, he thought; I feel I had lost something, something dear, yet I know not what at this moment. Jim sped through the length of the tunnel as the Jaguar shifted into high gear. He raced up onto Government, then over to Springhill, narrowly missing detection by a local police officer. Jim drove on to Park Place, turning right to leap up the drive, wanting so badly in his heart to find Mary, to see Mary, to tell Mary that he hoped everything was fine for her, because he was worried that he would lose her somehow. He jumped out of the car and ran up the red brick steps toward the main floor, crossing the front threshold as the car's engine ran on in the drive.

Mary! Mary!, Jim called out. She did not answer. She was not lounging in the parlor, deep in conversation with Anna, or eating the dining room, nor was she preparing food in the kitchen. Jim climbed up the main staircase, but Mary was not reading, or working in the library, nor was she napping in the master bedroom. She was not bathing or dressing, so he ran up the next staircase, but she was not tidying the guest room, nor was she in the other bedrooms. He ran up the last set of stairs to the attic, but she was not there, either. Jim was so frustrated that he let himself float right through the ceiling of the attic out to the sky above.

Where are you Mary!, he called out. But she did not respond. Slowly, he let himself come down into the attic; he solemnly stepped down to the floor below, letting his energy and mood fall as he descended the stairs, then down to the middle floor, as his emotions fell, then back down to the main floor, while he landed his mind on the hardwood floor.

All Jim could do was sit down onto his knees, with his face in his hands, but he continued trying to figure out what happened to Mary. But he saw a curious object on the foyer table a few steps away; it was a tape recorder. Jim got onto his feet and picked it up, looking it over with widening eyes. It must have a message on it, he thought; so he pressed play, which began to reveal its secret.

My dearest Jim, Mary's voice said on the tape, I have gone away, to search for my self; blood instantly rushed through Jim's neck, flushing his face with redness; I have never wanted to hurt you, but I needed to get away from you for a while, so I can sort some things out. I am deeply sorry to hurt you now, but I must look after my own mental health and not be bound only by my love for you. I have not made any plans for my future, but I now know it has been irrevocably changed. I do love you. Goodbye.

Jim's ears began to ring louder and louder as he put the recorder back down onto the table. He sat down onto the floor of his house, slightly stumbling, finally rolling back and lying out stretched, flat on his back. He gazed blankly at the room around him, looking at nothing, while seeing everything. His eyes floated high, away from him, allowing his soul to twirl, boundless, removed from the supine body below, soaring deep within the haze of emotion which clouded the room for him now, and as he found himself floating, he felt he was in search of a shape and direction for his thoughts...

...Your father has gone away, Jimmy, Elizabeth Mercer had said to Jim.

Yes, he thought, remembering.

Your father has gone to a lovely place, she

added, as she sat on the leather sofa in the library.

Jim's levitating soul took him there, back to when he was only fourteen, as he stood by the window, where his desk is now, with his back to his Mother. She suddenly began to weep into her hands without control.

And...he misses you, she stuttered under her tears. Mrs. Mercer rose and quickly left Jim alone in the library. Jim's body stood alone, absolutely still, and his mouth was slightly open, as he turned and gazed in the direction of the open door.

But, what do you mean, he has gone away, he asked, where has he gone, why did he leave? Jim turned, rather mechanically, toward the window and slowly walked closer to it. He put his small fingers onto the pane and looked out at the leaves as they were rustling on their trees and the cars as they were wisping by on their street. His eyes now became wider as he took in the whole of the scene before him, detailing each instance of movement beyond the plane of the window. It is all moving, Jim thought, all moving somewhere, but where? Where did he go? When is he coming back? Can I go there? Where is he!...

...Bye-bye Jimmy, Thomas Mercer said, with his hand on the doorknob of the garage, for he was getting tired, and thought that Jimmy should work on the project by himself. He stood tall, wearing wingtips, stubs, a starched shirt, and a pulled out tie.

What?, Jim said, you can't leave!

Why not?

Because you have to help me.

I do?

The racer, Jim pleaded to his father, the racer

needs work. I can't do it by myself.

Jimmy; you must do it by yourself; it was your project, your design and your engineering; I haven't helped you with anything but the building, anyway, so I'm sure you can work your problems out and win the Derby next month. Jim looked back at his soapbox racer, with its nose painted with flames, and felt a gentle push from his father. A sudden rush of emotion came over him and he thought; maybe I can do it!, I'll crush those guys with my design!

Okay Dad, I think I understand, Jim said, newly charged with excitement.

I'll be here for you, son, every step of the way, but you can do it. I'm going to bed now though, it's late, and I haven't felt to well the past couple of days. Goodnight Jimmy, he said as he stepped outside.

Goodnight Dad, Jim said, looking back on the mess of parts on the workbench.

Thomas Mercer coughed into his fist as he shut the door of the garage, which had been taken over by Jim, in designing his racer. I hope I get to see the Derby, he thought, for time is fast running out for me now. What am I doing?, he asked himself; keeping this from Elizabeth and Jimmy? They will be better off for not having worried about what they can't control. Mr. Mercer continued to roll the guilt over and over in his mind as he walked along the stone path toward the back door of the house, while coughing a few times into his hand and periodically looking up at the sky.

Jim eyed his racer and thought about being inside its cockpit, screaming his way downhill with the wind blowing in his face; with everyone else left behind and only he out front, slicing the air before him as he rolls across the line a victor...

...That's the way it's going to have to be, he thought, still standing in the library, gazing out the window. That's the way it will be, for Dad. I'll win this one for him. Jim looked out at the leaves and cars and people; he let his eyes rise higher to the bigger oaks, higher to the tops of the trees; still higher to the thinly clouded sky. What would it be like to fly up there, he thought. I could just swim around up there, looking at everything...; but a loud crash interrupted his thoughts; again, it crashed. Jim looked straight up and out the window to see that it was the old wooden shutter outside the guest room which was slamming against the outside wall, stirred on by the breeze. His floating eyes were tired and looked no longer on things beyond the glass...

Jim could not avoid looking one more time at the boat house as he walked by, with its door still swinging back and forth, banging against the door frame. He slowly made his way up to the house, with his sensibilities duly numbed from the trauma, his awareness surely narrowed; he opened the large glass back door and stepped into the den, allowing himself to fall into the leather chair in the corner. Jim sat motionless for minutes on end while gazing flat and blankly out away from himself.

Perhaps it was only a mirage, he thought, perhaps it was only an image somehow drawn from a nightmarish conception I had; maybe it was only a phantasm born from some such fantastical notions long ago sublimated. It was not, indeed he admitted, a phantom of the brain, or an illusion, or a *trompe l'oeil*, or even an appearance. Why must I have been forced by Mary to view such outlandish imagery? Did she think that some function was served by enslaving my long subjugated vision; what a cruel task mistress she is to be appeased by coercing me into her tribunal of sheer folly! I should think this to be some kind of a trick, but the vision of her body itself had the very bent of reality. I cannot therefore discount my own eyes, even though such a dismissal would better suit my mental health! These ideas, however, will only lead me down a path of sorrow which will infinitely repeat its route. My wife is now gone; her tearful voice has been silenced, and her insulated mind has been released into the void of the spheres; I am forced to be here to witness only the pale afterimage of her life.

...Mary had slammed the front door of the Mobile house behind her, but Jim caught it, as he chased, coming in after her.

I don't want to talk about it, Jim!

You have to talk about it!

No!, she screamed as she ran up the staircase and into the library.

Mary, do you know how much I love you?

No! You don't love me; you shouldn't love me, she said, becoming tearful, as she sat on the sofa. Jim sat down softly beside her.

I love you, he said, as plainly and directly as he knew how. He knew that he loved her unconditionally; that he would never stop loving her, he thought. Please don't shut me out, he said to himself. Please.

Oh, Jim, she said, beginning to allow him

closer. How can you be so nice, she thought, after what I have done to you? No!, she suddenly thought, though, and jumped to her feet, putting her face into her hands.

I don't deserve you, she whimpered, then sped out of the room. Jim leapt up and followed her. Mary!, he called. Mary, I...; he knew he could not find the words; he knew he could not find the thoughts to convey what he felt needed to be said. Mary fled back down the stairs with Jim in tow. She sped through the kitchen and out the back door, again slamming it, but it was stopped by Jim as he followed her out; out by the pool and onto the stone path, each step mounting more tension as they said nothing, as they both wondered what they could possibly say to each other. Mary reached the garage and started up the outside steps, which led to the studio above. She stepped up, yet slowed down, realizing she need not run any longer from Jim, for he was not chasing her; he was trying to comfort her. Why would I even want to run from him?, she thought. He followed her up, and they went into the studio, into the large open area in the center of the room.

Morning light from the windows, bouncing blue and gold from the northern sky streamed in through the pane glass, but left the wood paneled room rather dark, despite the influx of color. They stood looking on each other, silent, with the warm light draping their figures. They were both dressed for business and the warm rays highlighted all of their crisp, dark edges, as the frames of finished paintings Mary had lined along the walls were exposed. Mary found herself letting out a small nervous laugh and looked down at her heels briefly.

I feel like...I've let you down, she said, shaking, trembling with emotion.

I love you Mary, Jim returned, you haven't let me down, not one bit.

But I'm not...I can't give you, the doctor said...

Mary, I know how you must feel, Jim said as he moved closer to her; you feel that our long hopes for children have now been dashed, and maybe that is true, but, what you must understand is that my deep love for you overrides all of that. I love you Mary, and I always will, through the longest stretches, the deepest oceans of time, I will always love you.

I love you, Jim; she said quietly, as she allowed herself to cry again. Jim stepped closer and brushed her cheek with his hand, then embraced her with his arms. I love you, she said again, weeping. What if you lose me?, she added. Drying her eyes. What if...

I will never lose you, no matter what happens, you will always be here with me.

Mary closed her eyes and nodded a yes to him, she could relax now, she could let him love her even more than before, she could let herself love him more than was even possible before. I can't give him children, she thought, but he loves me more! I don't deserve this, and I don't deserve him. I love her, he thought, more than I knew I could, for even in this, I do not deserve her...

Jim got up onto his feet and wandered around the den of the beach house, looking through the teary eyes of a stranger at the oriental rug, the white leather sofa and chair, the bureau; he walked over to the

kitchen, around the slate marble topped island; out
through the dinning room, to the front door; then up the
staircase to the master bedroom and out on to the
balcony overlooking Perdido Bay. This house seems
strange to me now, he thought. He had not spent much
time in the house since Mary had moved into it. It
became her house during the last two weeks. Jim felt
as if he were intruding, somehow penetrating a
sanctuary, a scene where her soul was to be kept. This
was her private place for the last few moments of her
life, even though she was trying to sort her life and
future out; what became of it was the grief of her
existence; Jim suddenly felt that he must go away from
Mary's house; I must leave Mary in her tomb, he
thought, until another time. Another time, another time,
Jim repeated in his mind again and again as he walked
back down the stairs and out the front door. He walked
over to his black car, opened the door and sat down
inside; he stared at the gauges of the dashboard, looked
around at the white and black interior of the car, then
out the windscreen blankly. Jim was overwhelmed by a
feeling of being adrift on his own sea, for he was
painfully lost within a daze of twirling emotions.

Jim started the engine; the V-12 roared to life,
intake and exhaust tuned to the consumption of time.
He eased the transmission into gear and began to move
the car down the drive, away from the house.   Jim
thought that the car now pierced the shattered remains
of his projected future, as it rolls along the tangent line
of time, of future development spurred by Mary's
suicide. It was as if he had lost his past, erased his
memory and lacked all experience, he thought.

There was now, for Jim, no childhood spent in Mobile, playing in the backyard of the Springhill house, no mother and father; Father had not died when he was fourteen; he had not gone off to college at Vanderbuilt; he never met Mary Louis in that bookstore in Fairhope, nor did they marry; there was no beach house and there was no *Ideal*. The only time which remained for Jim was the time within the immediate circumstance, within his prison inside the rolling automobile. The car was now only a transport across a matrix which continually disappeared behind the car as it rolled, revealing only the immediate part of the structure to come. My past has vanished into thin air, Jim thought, and all which remains is the presence, the pounding ardor of the moment. It projects itself into an uncharted, and thus, opaque future. The circuitous path of temporality, which is represented by the car's rolling presence, leads me into that labyrinthian realm which does not privilege any particular line of time, but totalizes them all into a singular unity; into a mishmash of strange and competing times, all formed by the whirling of these random tangentials; such is the prison, the one on which I am now forced to travel. It is a *falsetto* of the moment, and a directionless kind of tack by which I only filter, into what is to be, for me, a silent domain.

What of our future?, Jim asked himself. The plans we had envisioned are, of course, no more; they have been abruptly shattered by this terrible deed. Now, it is Mary's last moment of time which marches on, into the future, secured upon its tangential line, traveling through the slit of a dreadful rupture. I am now being pulled, whether I like it or not, down a

timeline which was initiated by Mary; she is my sole
task mistress now, she has thus cursed me and sent me
reeling along her tangent, without the merest
knowledge of where I will land.

As Jim fell prey to the tyranny of the moment,
and as he began forgetting both he and Mary's past, and
their future together, which now lay deeply in ruin, he
found silenced within his memory the powerful
projection of his life which he had always known, for it
was met swiftly by its inverse power. Jim drove on,
though, letting the Jaguar spin him from Sandy Point at
Orange Beach, where Mary's body hung, through the
flat and lush country of 'Pleasure Island', toward the
bright coast of Gulf Shores. It was the only place
which came to mind where he might allow himself a
respite from the internal pressure of Mary's death.

Anna Lipscomb was flying, up high over the
green ocean, far up into the purple sky, as it lay shining
with its many yellow stars, when down upon the hot
orange sand of the beach in front of her white house,
she saw her friends, Jim and Mary, who stood opposed
to each other. They looked up at Anna as she flew and
waved to her, so she descended down to the beach, not
too far from the crashing green waves, which gave off a
lime foam. She came down to the beach and flew right
in between them, standing between Jim and Mary, in an
attempt to see both of them at the very same time,

continually looking back and forth from one to the other as she tried to develop the *Janus* face which would allow her to accomplish this feat. Mary grabbed one of her hands and Jim grabbed the other; they began to tug on Anna's arms, pulling her hard in both directions as she looked at them with a puzzled face. Suddenly she split into two Anna's, with two faces, and both Jim and Mary had a version of her. On Jim's side, Anna looked at herself; she looked at Mary and herself as they faded from sight. What is happening?, she dreamt. She was afraid that the version of her with Jim, and Jim as well, would fade. What is happening?, she dreamt in fear. Then the entire scene faded as Anna began to swim up from her deep sleep; she slowly roused herself; she opened her slightly green eyes and began to stretch her long arms; she looked up at the ceiling for a few minutes, and was unable to avoid thinking about what she had just been dreaming.

Anna rose late in the mornings, as she had been usually consumed on the nights before with a project or two in her studio. But this morning she remembered that there was a reason she should have wanted to get up a bit earlier, but she had forgotten it, so did not set her alarm. She stood up from the large bed, throwing off the white sheet and comforter from her nude figure, which was made a soft camel color by the high key light which came through the white house, and filled the bedroom, even with the blinds drawn tight. Anna walked out of the bedroom, crossing the hallway and stepped into the large dark studio. She put on the lights, which brought filled the room and brought the huge sculpture to life, which sat in the middle of the room. It was nearly seven feet tall, and had its mass made up of several pieces of metal and plastic filler. Its many jagged arms reached out from the center at eccentric angles. Anna stood looking at her sculpture, which was already a collage made from many strange and various elements, and this was before even being subjected to her camera's eye. It was, as she thought, nearly ready for the lighting and shooting, which would thereby begin the stage of photographic manipulation, and, though she was still weighing out the many possibilities of the presentations she could pursue, she well knew that in the end, she would go forward with pure instinct and never look back to question it.

Suddenly, she remembered what it was that she was to do this morning. She remembered that, a couple of days ago, Mary had asked her to drop by the beach house and have lunch today; she walked quickly out of the studio, flicking off the lights, which threw the great sculpture into obscurity again, and stepped around through the hallway to the massive living room, which was bathed in day long light from the very large glass panels and doors which covered all three walls and offered an overlook, across a polished metal balcony, at the Gulf of Mexico. Anna was looking around, searching for her daytimer. It lay closed on the other side of the great room on the glass dining table; she walked across the white marble tile floor and picked up the small black booklet; she opened it to the current day and it read, 'lunch w/Mary 11ish'.

I guess I'm going to be late, she thought, as she glanced over to the clock's hands on the wall of the white kitchen. She then looked out to the deep blue seawater of the Gulf, as its surf rolled over and over, foaming white, in its reach for the bright, white sand. The full light of late morning from outside poured into the sheer ivory house, and fell then upon Anna; it poured into her deep brown, shoulder length hair and revealed that it had strong red highlights, her hazel eyes revealed the flecks of green in them and her face had a sharp, but pale quality, with a hint of freckle. She was resolutely happy, and quite youthful, for a grown woman of twenty-nine; she was still as full of bright wonder as any child.

Looking down at herself, enjoying her tall, slim body which was draped within the white light, she thought for a minute about taking a long bath, but she had bathed the afternoon before, and realized her promise to Mary for a lunch date, so she quickly turned and went back across the large room to the hallway, then into the bedroom, and into the closet. She put on the light and began to leaf through her wardrobe, finally to pick out a silver silk blouse and black wool skirt; she took up a pair of black sandal heels and switched off the light. She threw the clothes onto the bed and went into the bathroom; in front of the mirror she brushed her teeth, put on a bit of lipstick and primped her hair lightly, pausing for a moment to examine her face; she then went back to the bed and slipped into the blouse, taking just a moment to comically grab her breasts in a large gesture and dance around for a few seconds while she hummed a melody. She buttoned her blouse and stepped into the skirt while humming along, pulling the skirt up to secured it with its shiny black belt. Anna continued her dance, twirling her tall body within the tickling comfort of the blouse, which fit loosely, and the shapely skirt, which hugged her hips tightly, cut well above the knee and slit up the back; she put on the sandal heels, then let herself fall back onto the bed like a rag doll, thinking again about the sculpture in the studio, imagining again various versions of a print, yet completely satisfied with none of them.

Cutting off her thoughts abruptly, realizing again the time, she jumped up, grabbed her small, black leather purse, fumbled for her keys, and headed out to the hallway, toward the front door. Before she reached the door, though, she turned off to walk across the bright sun porch, through the kitchen, and to the dining table again, where she had left the daytimer; she picked it up and put it in her purse, then stepped back through the kitchen, the sun porch, then to the door. She glided down the steps which led from the storm safe level of the beach house to the driveway and poured herself into the black BMW, throwing her purse onto the floor of the passenger side. She started up the engine and put down the top, then peeled out on the concrete drive on her way to the road. Highway 182 led eastward from her house, just outside Gulf Shores, to 161 northward, then she pulled on to Canal Road, which runs along the Intracoastal Waterway, arriving only just moments after Jim had passed by, going the other way.

Her hair waved in the wind as she drove; she wore black rimmed sunshades which she had found recently in Rome; the wind played with her silver blouse, tickling her skin as she sped down the road; she left the radio off, and each time ran through the gears with joy, while taking in the air of late morning. What a beautiful day, she thought, the sky is a deep blue, dotted with big, puffy clouds. The Sun is beaming down, making everything smell so wonderful. I love the sound of the engine and the exhaust, the sound of tires on the road...that is a lovely new house they are building! It looks as if there is a sun porch on that one side. That is great. I love my sun porch at home. Maybe Mary will want to have a picnic lunch out on the grass by the bay; I'm not in the mood for the usual restaurants.

Anna made her way toward the Mercer beach house in no particular hurry, but for hunger. She even stopped on the side of the road a couple of times, and, pulling a camera out of the glovebox, would do a spot photograph of a flower, or take note of another house. She would stand and stare intently at the bush or house, taking in all of the color and texture it could offer her, she would then fire the camera, then turn, fully delighted, and move back to the car, remembering each time that she was late for her lunch with Mary. She would take off from the side of the road and run through the gears once again, just as completely amused as before and finally settle the car down into a comfortable, and legal, speed.

A few minutes later, and thoroughly behind schedule, she drew up to the Mercer beach house. She parked right behind Mary's gray Mercedes and left the top down. Taking a moment to check herself in the rearview mirror before getting out of the car, she paused to think about what they could eat, for Mary would never decide on her own. She got out of the car and stepped across the sea shell and gravel drive, moving toward the front door of the house, as she ran her fingers through her hair, and as she looked out to the blue water of the bay and the light green trees and shrubbery on both sides of its shores. As she made it up to the door and grabbed for the knob, she noticed the door of the boat house as it slowly swung ajar, pushed by the wind. Anna looked at it for an instant, but shoved the door open, realizing that she did not need her key, for the door was unlocked, as usual.

Mary?, she called out as she closed the door, adding, I'm here. She heard nothing. Alright, she said, I know the car is here, where are you? She walked through the dining room, noticing the bottle and glasses, and went by the wet bar and into the kitchen. She saw, across the den, the black stockings and high heels on the sofa.

Hmmm, this looks interesting, a night of debauchery, she said under her breath while walking across the spread of the den to the sofa, where she sat down and took up one of the stockings; she thought about Mary wearing these and began to imagine her dressed for their lunch together wearing a long black velour dress, unbuttoned up to the thigh, with the stockings and heels. Anna imagined Mary teasing her with her outfit as they ate lunch, forcing her to wait as long as possible to get her hands underneath that dress, and onto Mary's body. Anna rubbed the stocking on her cheek and sniffed it, thinking about Mary's sweet perfume, then put it down and looked around the room nervously, hoping Mary would show up soon.

Maybe she is upstairs, she thought, perhaps washing off whatever it was that happened last night.

Anna stood and walked toward the stairs, climbed them to the top, pausing to look at the photograph of Mary which Jim had taken. Anna pulled herself away from the photograph and went into the bedroom, calling for Mary. She then went to look in the bathroom, then returned to the hallway again, and went on to the other bedroom, but then returned only a moment later; she walked back into the master bedroom and over to the open glass doors on the balcony and leaned on the metal rail, making herself relax as the wind gently played with her hair and face. Anna stood staring at the water and sky, thinking about how beautiful it all seemed to her. It is really a super nice day, she thought, and wished that she could eat soon; she could have a nice lunch with Mary on the grass.

Where are you Mary?, she said aloud, beginning to get flustered. She then heard the engine of a small aircraft circling far above in the sky, and then it came into full view for her, as it was running along the shoreline just a few miles away. The plane was pulling behind it a billboard, and Anna thought that perhaps the pilot was making his way around to run back across the shoreline toward Gulf Shores. What does the billboard say?, she thought; I can just make it out. *Pink Pony Pub*. Of course, I know that place, but it says something else; I can't make it out, though, oh well. The plane slid across the sky toward the West and slowly went out of sight and earshot for Anna. She continued to lean on the balcony rail and stare out at the world, taking it in with all of the delight she could, as she waited patiently for Mary to reemerge from wherever she has been.

Jim looked up into the southeastern sky, staring off at the depth of the firmament, and then noticed the aircraft moving across the beach, silently, towing a sign. He was standing on the East Beach at Gulf Shores, and the wind prevented him from hearing the plane as it approached. He stood with his hands inside the pockets of his pants, and feeling the sand between his toes, for he had left his shoes and blazer in the car, and had unbuttoned his shirt, pulled the tail out and rolled up his sleeves, for even though it was not hot on this day, he wanted to let everything go, to give up his usual professional appearance.

He had walked onto the sand and stopped mid-stride to watch the plane as it unfolded its path toward the western horizon. Is it a line that now is scribed by this craft?, he thought; a line between two kinds of spaces; or is it a vector plainly through the depth of a three-dimensional space? Is it a border which serves to divide two spaces, defining an 'either/or,' when what I see in the sky is a lonely projectile drawing an internal vector; a bullet piercing the *One*; a moment pushing itself into the future? Perhaps it is neither; maybe it is only a stupid airplane gliding by with a shameless advertisement for a dip and dive?

I could run, he thought. I could run fast across this beach and attempt to pierce the *One* all by myself. I could then see what it is which is on the other side of this moment.

Just then Jim lit up from where he was comfortably standing and began to run in his full stride. He began to race the plane across the beach to the West with all of the speed he could muster. His long legs reached and grabbed the sand, using his feet, which dug into the sand, and propelled him forward, throwing small spays of sand out from behind his feet as they churned through. His heart and lungs began to pump pure energy as he lunged through each long stride. The wind now roared into his ears and made his eyes tear up as he leapt. He ran past the condominiums on the East Beach, he ran past *Youngs*, past the *Pink Pony Pub* and past the Pavilion.

Jim was racing, and pushing hard against the *One* as the plane followed above. Each step left a little bit of the moment behind as Jim sprinted in the noon-time Sun. But he thought that, perhaps, it was the Sun he was racing, and he would not give up, for to beat the Sun was to never allow it to set, to never let it cease in its function of providing visibility for the intelligible parts of the *One*. Perhaps it was Mary he was running away from; for in the shock and terror of finding her dead, he had fallen into a feeling of despair and anger at her; to leave her secure within her moment was to let night fall upon her life as he raced toward the forever long day of his. So Jim ran and ran, his eyes tearing both from the wind and from his pain; he ran within the section of time and space which lay between Mary and the Sun. Jim quickly began to tire, however, and he was forced to face the possibility that his dream would fade, that the Sun would set after all, and the plane would continue to cross the firmament uninfluenced by his desire. Jim's body gave out and he was forced to stop, before collapse. The dream was now gone, but Jim marvelled at how great a distance he had covered, since he had not been running lately.

As he caught his breath, bent over with his hands on his knees, Jim began to feel thirsty and wondered what he could do about a drink. He felt the back of his trousers for his wallet and looked around, noticing a favorite spot; *B.J.'s Seafood* was not far off. As he made his way toward the restaurant, he made a small effort to straighten his shirt, to tuck in its tail and he wiped his face off with his hands. As he approached the restaurant, he could hear the airplane circling for a run back across the beach. Jim reached the steps of *B.J.'s* and started up them, but paused to look at the plane as it began its run in the eastern direction. He watched it for a moment as it glided along the shore, then he turned back toward the restaurant, and climbed the last remaining steps to the door.

Anna stood with pursed lips and crossed eyebrows studying the contents of the refrigerator, wondering what she could get away with eating, while not spoiling her, now late, lunch with Mary. She grabbed an apple and took a bite out of it, still perusing the other contents and she looked around as she closed the refrigerator door, continuing to whittle the apple down. As she ate, Anna nosed around in the kitchen, restless and bored, and began opening cabinets, looking inside, then closing them, unaffected by their contents; she danced across the linoleum, shaking her hips, and pretending to be singing on a stage, then went over to the wet bar and fiddled with the bottles and glasses. Her eyes took her into the den, still dancing, then the parlor, where she sat down into a leather high-back chair, crossing her legs and swinging her foot, then jumped up and moved over to the sofa, sitting in a grand fashion, as if she wore a full bodice, petticoat and dress. No sooner was she settled when she leapt up and began to waltz with an imaginary suitor across the room and into the foyer. Her steps were arrested while she was taken by the small black and white photograph of Jim and Mary. Anna took another bite from the apple she had carried with her all this time; I got them just right, she thought, smiling herself as she gazed into their still eyes, as she smiled in concert with them. Anna then spun herself around and did a showgirl step, but then left it incomplete as she walked casually over into the dining room; she picked up the wine bottle and glasses from the dining room table and took them to the kitchen. Then she emptied the remains of the wine down the drain and put the bottle in the garbage and placed the glasses inside the dishwasher. After finishing the apple, she placed the core in the garbage as well.

Once again, Anna became bored with waiting, and, in a glance from the kitchen to the sofa in the den, she noticed again the stockings and heels; she walked over to the sofa and looked at the stockings, while trying to figure out what she could get away with. After thinking for a moment, Anna kicked off her sandal heels and pulled her skirt up over the bare skin of her hips; she sat down on the sofa, then slipped one of the black silks up the length of her lightly sun-browned left leg, pulling the black lace band tight, up to the very top of her thigh. She slipped the second silk onto her other leg and stepped into the black stilettos, caressing her legs, turning and flexing the muscles, rubbing one leg against the other, and complementing

herself on how well the new additions worked with her
outfit.   Anna began to fantasize about Mary; she
thought about her blonde hair, done in a new perm, her
breasts, exposed as she unbuttoned the black velour
dress, and her legs, covered in the same black silk Anna
was now wearing; Anna began to masturbate with her
right hand, invisible between her thighs, and her left
hand tucked behind her head as she kicked and bent her
legs.

She fantasized that Mary had just walked in.
She could come in just now, right this moment as I am
getting off, she thought, to catch me fingering myself
with her stockings and heels on.   Mary struts over in
her black outfit, going over toward Anna, and then gets
down onto her knees, kissing Anna's legs, up to the
inside of her thighs.   She then leans back and takes off
her dress, showing Anna that she is naked underneath,
and begins to eat Anna out as Anna squeezes her
breasts.   Anna screamed briefly as she achieved her
quick climax and then lay back staring at the painted
ceiling momentarily.   No such luck, she thought, Mary
missed it this time.   I'll have to save that fantasy for a
later day, maybe even later today.

Anna stood up with her new accents on, and,
feeling only slightly embarrassed, even though nobody
was around, pushed the skirt back over her exposed
groin, buttocks and hips; she walked around the house
feeling the play of her legs as they rubbed against the
silks, then, feeling restless, went out to the front door,
and stepped outside, looking down and noticing that her
legs were shiny in the sunlight and that the stilettos
made her quite tall.   She wished that Mary would show

up soon and see her in her outfit, for she knew that Mary always liked Anna to be dressed up, and she wouldn't mind at all if Anna was wearing some of her things.

Anna decided to keep moving, searching for some way to pass time, so she strutted down to the dock and walked down its length to reach the boat and, leaning on the safe lines, called for Mary, then for Jim, thinking he may be on board, as she kicked up her left leg behind her, feeling very sexy. Not a soul responded to her calls. She turned away from the boat as the wind blew her hair against her cheeks and her blouse against her skin, then walked back to the end of the dock, and, spying the boat house, decided there may be something to play with inside, since she had ignored it until now.

With its door moving slightly back and forth in the wind, the boat house looked positively mysterious to Anna, as she then stepped up to the door and lightly pushed it open, calling again for Mary, for Jim, for anybody who might be inside. Anna then was struck squarely between her eyes by a poignant shock, she saw Mary's still body before her, dead and hanging from the wooden ceiling by a long white rope; Anna then felt the shock run through her entire body; she was speechless and only stood as still as Mary was, with her mouth open. Mary's face and neck were, in the light of the boat house, purple, having been hanging now for more than three hours; her body was unclothed and absolutely still. Anna's gaze was frozen upon the body in front of her, and even though she was profoundly disturbed, she began to feel a powerful sting of anger at Mary.

Why did you do this!, she yelled at Mary, I've been waiting around and you were hanging out here! You bitch!, Anna screamed, you stupid bitch!, why did you do it!?; we were supposed to have lunch, she said, more quietly, and with a rush of tears. Mary, she said, as she whimpered; I love you, why did you do it? Anna began to cry, and she cried as freely as she knew how, as freely as she had cried as a child, in an uninhibited manner, undeterred by outer forces; she walked over, close to the body, which hung two feet off of the floor, and touched Mary's right hand, then hugged Mary's body with her head against Mary's belly. The body was only cold and silent, and, of course, provided absolutely no engagement, in any way whatsoever for Anna, who desperately needed for Mary to speak to her.

Jim had emerged, then, from B.J.'s well-watered and a bit groggy, having been up late, awake early, and then...; the sight of Mary...dead! As he walked back toward the Jaguar, he decided that a nap was only in order, but probably would be a quite unavoidable consequence. However, he thought that the authorities should be involved in the incident of this morning, but felt that, since so much time had gone by already, it could probably wait until after he had napped a bit. Nevertheless, Jim made it to the car, got in, and drove off; and he kept driving, as he was beginning to worry a bit more about Mary's body and what the authorities may require from him; what they would ask of him; doubtless there were people who saw him out on the bay this morning...there could be talk of murder, but someone must have seen him sailing...it could be quite a mess to deal with. He therefore stayed on his course toward the beach house, going back along by the beach this time, past Anna's house to the crossroad, then to Sandy Point at Orange Beach.

Anna stepped back from the dangling body, realizing that she would get no kind of emotion from it, and looked at it blankly as she continued to step back, coming to rest against the door frame. I do not believe it, she thought, I just can't believe it, I don't...she's dead. Mary is dead, and her body is hanging coldly from the neck inside this dank room. Anna remembered her audacious sexuality from only minutes before, and, after feeling guilty about it for a moment, she began to become strangely aroused. She somehow felt that Mary was, indeed, watching her as she masturbated inside, and she wondered what Mary thought about it. But, feeling the possibility of a certain pathological association which would not be based upon any reality, Anna thought to herself; I've got to get away from this for a moment.

She walked out of the boat house, and back up to the front door of the beach house. She made a beeline straight from the front door, through the dining room, to the wet-bar; she opened the cabinet, and saw a bottle of gold tequila, pulled it out and poured a shot into a glass, which was nearby. Anna gulped the shot down, feeling the sting of the alcohol in her throat, and then poured herself another shot, which she gulped too. Anna then put the bottle away and walked over to the large glass door in the den, at the back of the house, and set immediately to looking out and away at the trees, at the water, in an attempt to think about nothing in particular. Anna found herself feeling the obvious effects of the recent and disturbing event; she could not avoid feeling the reverberation of shock throughout her body.

Jim made it to the drive of the house as Anna stood looking out of the glass. He saw Anna's car and pulled up behind it. He was glad to see that she was here, but had no way of knowing if she had found Mary, or was in the dark about the matter. He got out of the car and sauntered toward the house, not knowing what to expect; making it up to the door, he quietly opened it; he slipped inside and saw Anna standing at the glass door through the foyer; she immediately turned and saw Jim.

Anna, he said.

Jim.

Were you supposed to meet Mary today?

Yes, tentatively, she smirked.

I don't think she's going to make it.

No. I agree. I really don't think she will be here either.

Anna, I take it you...you have been out to the boat house?

Yes. Yes, I went down there.

I see.

Jim, I...; she stopped cold, unable to speak the feeling inside. Jim rushed across the room and took Anna up into his arms; they embraced for a few silent moments, then they began to kiss each other.

I haven't seen you for a week, Anna said.

I've been busy. Actually, I haven't been busy, I've been a little morose, I needed some time to myself after, well, after Mary left me.

I don't know what to do, Anna winced.

About...

About Mary. They both became still as the shock returned to their awareness.

I'll call the authorities in time, Jim said, showing a little discomfort; I just do not want them crawling all over the place right now.

When did she...

I came over last night to talk, she had been gone for two weeks, we drank some wine, and...

I can figure that out, Anna said, fondling his shirt buttons.

Well, this morning we argued a little, and I went out to sail out in the bay, I got back about nine-thirty, and...there was...it was the most disturbing sight of my life.

For me too, I have never seen a body before. It was a bit exhilarating.

Jim looked around the room, noting Anna's sandals over by the sofa; he then looked at her outfit, down at her legs and shoes. I see you changed your clothes, he said as he rubbed her hips and kissed her neck.

Not really, I, uh, I was bored, waiting for Mary...not knowing where she was... Anna was lulled by Jim's charisma into fantasy. She fell enraptured for a moment by his aura and began to get excited.

I see, Jim said, now massaging Anna underneath

her wool skirt. Anna interrupted her fall and stepped away, though, from Jim, looking a bit confused, and pulled her skirt back down, showing an uncommon amount of modesty; she walked past him toward the door, imagining that she could drive away and leave him here alone, but she walked slow enough to let him follow her, imagining that he would chase her anywhere, and that they would have a lurid affair. She strutted her body like a supermodel, allowing her fantasies to take her over, for she found that sex, driven by fantasy was the height of pleasure; Jim lurked behind her, watching her legs, and as they reached the door, Anna opened it and Jim pinned her against it, kissing her all over her neck, but Anna pushed him away, playing the offended lover, and went outside.

The wind caught their hair and clothing, as Jim followed her lead toward the boat house, putting aside, for the moment, who was hanging within. They reached the door and went inside, and Jim, struck fully again by the shock of death, stood staring at the body, dead and naked, stunned momentarily. Anna, shocked as well, but hiding it, slammed the door shut behind him but he did not notice; she unbuttoned her blouse as he looked at the body. Jim turned around, hearing, though delayed, the slam of the door, and looked on Anna and she opened her blouse, pulling the tail out of her skirt, to reveal her breasts, whose nipples were extremely hard; she ran her hand up the inside of his thigh to reach his groin, and his erection thickened in her hand.

Make love to me, she said, before kissing him with her tongue.

The deeply erotic clamor of her being and the allure of taboo sang largely to Jim. His inhibitions were easily let go and he grabbed her by the shoulders and pushed her against the door; he kissed her neck and breasts as Anna squeezed his harder on his erection. He moved her to the workbench nearby and sat her up on it; he unbuttoned his trousers and let them fall to the wooden floor; she pushed her skirt up over her hips, revealing her crotch to him. He positioned himself between her legs as she crossed them behind him, and inserted his thick erection into her receptive body. Anna roared with excitement as she looked at Mary's body behind Jim; he started to push and slam harder into her, pounding her into the shelving behind her, rattling tools and paint cans as she screamed. Anna reached her second orgasm, and as Jim was ready to break, they both screamed loudly, over and over as they each came on each other. Jim, though, kept pushing as Anna continued to moan, and he began to come again, rubbing Anna's silky legs and kissing her breasts as he dripped sweat onto her stomach. Their tiring bodies gradually came to a halt as they slowly caught their breath; beginning to kiss with open mouths, while caressing each other's body.

I love you Anna.

I love you too, she said, then looked at Mary, but I miss Mary.

I do too, he said, looking at the body, turning around to lean onto the bench. Anna massaged his shoulders as he sat in front of her, staring at Mary, allowing his soul to lift, taking in a higher and higher awareness. Jim let his thoughts drift to other moments.

...Can you catch me Jimmy?, Jim heard in the distance.

Can you catch me?, he heard again as the voice became close; as his awareness descended quickly onto the grassy yard by the lagoon.

Jimmy! Can you catch me?, Cindy Winfield had called, motioning to Jim to chase her across the yard. It was all the entertainment the children needed at that age of eight.

I can catch you, Jim returned, knowing that he would have to pretend to be winded, pretend that he couldn't quite chase her down, when it was an easy task for him. He could effortlessly run her down in three or four strides, but as she jumped away, running for her life, as it seemed to her, away from Jim, he only put on a show of a chase.

Cindy ran across the yard and into the next yard, laughing with nervous excitement as Jim tracked her course; her flaxen blonde hair rippled in the wind and her sun dress billowed within the air.

You can't catch me!, Cindy teased. You can't catch me! You can't catch me! She ran around the houses, between their stilts and back around through the yards toward the house Thomas and Beth Mercer had rented.

You're getting tired!, Jim sang, and I'm gonna catch you!

No, you're not!

Yes, I am! I'm gonna catch you!, he sang.

Cindy stopped near the stilts of the Mercer house and bent over to breathe hard; her heart raced and her face was red.

Man, you can run fast, Jim announced, feigning exhaustion, bending over as Cindy had.

I've gotta go home, she said.

Me too, Jim returned.

Cindy stepped over to Jim and pecked him on the cheek with all the tenderness of a fully blossomed woman and promptly skipped off toward home. Jim went upstairs and fell into a nap on his bed near the open window, its curtains swayed by the gentle breeze coming through them. There was a noise which interrupted his pleasure, though, it's that shutter, he figured, which continues to slap the wall, as he recalled. Bang. Bang. When will it stop? Why won't someone go up there and stop it? Why do we have to listen to it. Where has my Dad gone? Why did he have to leave me standing here, listening to this stupid shutter? Why can't I go back to the beach again, and nap on the bed with the sea air coming in?...

...But then he heard Mary calling him. She was calling him from all the way down on the first floor as he hurried to straighten up the guest room. Jim's mother was coming soon to visit and check on things, driving from Fairhope, and he wanted the entire house to sparkle. He could hear a city bus roaring, down at the corner, as Mary called for him again.

I'm way up here, he returned. In the guest room?, she thought.

I'm coming up she said. Jim couldn't wait to see her, he got excited just thinking about being alone in a room with her for a few minutes. Mary ascended the staircases like an angel floating on ether. I can't wait to see him, she thought. I am so nervous! I wish I could marry him today! She had made it to the last landing, and, looking down the banister, she could see how far she had climbed. Mary was nearly light-headed and stumbled helplessly into the guest room, just to sit for a minute; there was Jim. He caught her in his arms as her face turned red.

I love you, he said. Mary melted.

I love you too, she returned. He placed her on the bed and stretched her out so she could lie flat. I never wanted him to touch me so badly as I do now, she thought. They playfully kissed for a moment as Mary was slowly able to regain her composure.

Open the window, would you?, Mary asked. As he opened the window she kicked off her heels and stretched out a little more languidly on the bed. The breeze started to come in through the window, rustling the curtains and brushed Mary's silver silk dress across the fabric of her hose. I feel sexy, beautiful, she thought. Jim kicked off his loafers, pulled off his socks, and took off his shirt.

My pulse is rising faster and faster, she reported to him. I can imagine all kinds of scenarios unfolding from here, Jim.

What should I do first?, he asked.

What would be the most exciting thing to do?, Mary asked in return. Your mother isn't expected here for at least two more hours; we have all the time in the world. Jim got on top of Mary and pulled her dress up to uncover her stomach. He kissed her belly as she squirmed out of her underpants and hose, pushing them down with her feet as she tugged on Jim's belt and trousers. Jim pulled the dress up farther to expose

Mary's breasts and he kissed and licked her hardening nipples. Mary pulled her dress over her shoulders and threw it onto a nearby chair, which left them both nude. They continued to tease each other until Mary, not able to stand it any longer, grabbed Jim's erection and pulled him down onto her, allowing him to enter her moist body. She immediately had an orgasm as Jim moaned with pleasure. She then rolled him off of her, not feeling comfortable buried under him, and climbed on top of him, quickly reinserting him into her, as Jim kissed her dangling breasts. Only moments later, she was taken by another climax as Jim began to come inside her, and they both rocked the bed into the wall several times as they came. They settled down and Mary put her head down on Jim's chest as they both began to drift off. The shutter clapped and clapped outside against the wall, spurred on by the wind. The clouds flew overhead and the cars wisped by along the roadway...

        ...The long white sheer curtains blew out and away from the open double doors of the beach house and blew into the bedroom, making a playful rising and falling motion, carried by the wind. Jim was napping peacefully, yet was stirred up from sleep slowly by the sound of the early summer wind in the curtains. He rolled over and looked lustfully out through the sheer fabric, and began to remember those vacations with family as a boy, when he would play with Cindy and nap in the afternoon with the windows open. I was so carefree then, he thought. The play of the air and fabric on my bare skin was all the pleasure I needed in the world at that time. It was easy to be absolutely content with that feeling of luxury. Jim slowly opened his eyes to see the glass doors open to the balcony with their white curtains, and was surprised. He could not place himself.

Where am I, he erupted, as he leapt out onto the balcony and looked out into the scene with his sleepy eyes blinded by the brightness of the day. Oh. I see the bay, the boat house, this is our new retreat house at Orange Beach. Yes, of course. I can see Mary out there playing in the sand on the point. Mobile had become somewhat noisy and abrupt for Jim and Mary lately, and they thought that they could possibly find it easier to work where there were fewer interruptions...

...Anna, standing tall in her black satin evening dress, shook Mary's hand delicately, then took Jim's hand just as carefully. She had just arrived, from Gulf Shores, at the Mercer house for the show of Mrs. Mercer's paintings, as well as the cocktail party which went along with it, having been kept late at home, talking with clients. For such a long time, she thought, she had heard about Mary Louis-Mercer, she had seen a great deal of her work, and knew that to meet her would be an honor.

It is so nice to finally meet you both, Anna said.

So very good to meet you, Jim said, noticing Anna's sharp features in the warm light of the downstairs parlor.

Yes, indeed, Mary said; I have seen some of your drawing and painting over in Fairhope, Gulf Shores, and even here in Mobile. I have wanted to meet you for some time, for I have even had one of your prints put in our bedroom, she added, using a tone of complicity.

Really? Which one?...oh, you are the one!, Anna said with excitement, realizing that it was Mrs. Mercer who had ordered a huge enlargement of her Study in Summer, last year.

What do you mean?, Jim asked, not aware that Mary had ordered the print without a name.

Well, Mrs. Mercer had ordered the print anonymously, you see, Anna explained to Jim; and I never found out who it was. The one you ordered is the largest print I've done, it's one of my very favorites!

Mine too, Mary said, looking directly into Anna's eyes.

Please, show me your new work, Anna asked, lightly holding both hands on her champagne glass.

Oh, well, I have been dabbling in some new mediums over the years, Mary reported as she led Anna over to the wall, but I have gone back to plain old oil, if you can believe that. They stood before a complex work; an abstracted view of a kind of structure, in the style of a blueprint, which would, normally, be rendered in fine detail.

This is brilliant, Anna said; it looks to me like a skeleton of some building, but you have given it a blurry, sketchy quality, which negates the purpose of the blueprint.

There is definitely some kind of conflict going on here, Jim added.

Yes!, Anna agreed.

I wish I had your eye, Anna, Mary lamented; sometimes I feel that I am unable to say what I feel, and as I look at this work, I can tell that there is something missing.

You are far too critical of yourself, Anna said, attempting to reassure her, feeling now that the show and the party must have all been a bit too much for her sensibilities. Any vision I have, she carefully added, is a usefulness of the techniques I have been fortunate enough to learn from my teachers and from the various traditions.

Mary and Anna talked for several minutes as Jim listened on. Anna looked at Jim, and, in taking in his tall stature, his tan skin, his full, flowing hair and his smart tuxedo, she thought about what luck Mrs. Mercer must have had to have met this man years ago. Jim looked at Anna, and, as he noticed her youthful skin, her figure and her long, complex hair, he thought about what a breath of fresh air she was to him. It is not that he felt unhappy with Mary, he thought, but that there was something about her which was producing friction at present, and Miss Lipscomb did not seem to have this problem. She somehow represented more of his feminine ideal, for she held herself proudly, she was extremely sensitive, not only to her artistic vision, but to the needs of the people around her. She was absolutely beautiful, and also carried a sense of playfulness very close to the outer face of her personality.

Maybe we could meet for lunch one day, Anna?

Anna smiled from the very core of her being as the words were spoken to her, for she knew that this would be the pleasant beginning of something.

Mary, she responded, lunch would be great, I would be delighted if you could come over to my studio on the beach, and, if you like, we could have some cake and tea there. I have finished some work recently, which I haven't had the opportunity to show yet publicly.

I would be quite happy to visit, call me tomorrow and we'll set up a time next week. Mary then stepped over to a nearby bureau and slipped a calling card out of the drawer. It was a cream colored card and very plainly said '*Mrs. Mary Louis-Mercer*', and underneath there was a Mobile number and address. She stepped back to where Anna and Jim were standing and presented the card to Anna, smiling with an effortless face, and Anna took the card from her. Their fingers had touched each others' only briefly, one finger sliding against the other very gently, then Anna placed the card into her small, black purse. They shook hands once again, pausing for just a moment to focus on one another's eyes as Jim stood, silently watching on...

...As Mary's legs had spread, farther across the leather sofa, she began to moan as she stood backward on it, wearing only a black lace bra and fishnet stockings; underneath her, sitting forward on the sofa, was Anna, with her head buried into Mary's crotch. Anna was only wearing white high heels and a white lace boustier, and kept one hand between her own legs, as she fingered herself, and the other hand around Mary's leg. Mary continued to dance over Anna, thinking her to be her sole audience, but behind the double doors of the library, Jim was watching through the crack between them. He could not help getting turned on as he squeezed his erection in his pants. He could stand it no longer, for he was not offended, having caught them together; he was excited, for he wanted to join them. He had been attracted to Anna from the start and knew that this was his only opportunity to be with her.

He stood up and opened the doors. Mary and Anna froze in place, no knowing who it was. It was Jim, and nothing was said. Mary was scared that Jim would explode with anger at their affair and she could only stare at Jim and feel guilty. Mary slowly sat down onto Anna's lap, but then, she thought that maybe he would just leave them alone, if they continued. She gently put both hands around Anna's cheeks as she looked at Jim. Mary began to kiss Anna, licking her mouth, while they both glanced at Jim, who was staring intently at them, becoming more and more excited. He stepped into the room, slowly moving closer to them, exercising his visual lock on them. He walked around to the back of the sofa, facing Mary, and, as she continued to kiss Anna, faster and harder, he stepped in toward them. He grabbed Mary by the shoulders, pulling her near him. He ripped her bra off and squeezed her breasts, kissing her neck and chest as Mary began to moan with a new erotic pleasure. Anna returned to Mary's crotch, which sent Mary right into orgasm. Jim let her go, and moved around to the front of the sofa, taking off his shirt and stepping out of his trousers. He got down onto his knees and began kissing Anna's legs and feeling her breasts which were large, underneath the tight boustier. He leaned in and inserted his now throbbing erection into her wetness, causing her to scream loudly. They all exchanged couplings and became louder and faster as their mutual energy rose ever higher and higher...

...Jim and Anna had been napping, fully nude and peacefully, on the short beach of a small point far out in Perdido Bay. Their bodies lay exhausted, spent from a full day of sailing and sunbathing. A small boat had slowly approached them from some twenty yards off of the shore, but then settled into a course alongside the shore. A rifle was pulled out, and a shot fired across the distance. It had come very close to Jim and Anna, but had missed, only striking a small tree behind them. They both sat straight up, and were immediately blinded by the bright light in their eyes. The dark figure holding the rifle stood staring at them for an instant, before returning to the wheel of the boat. Jim gasped and shouted out at the figure.

Mary!

Oh shit, Anna said while reaching for her shirt.

As Jim stood up, the boat quickly sped off.

Oh my God, Jim said, stunned, and found that he could only sit back down as the veins on his neck pulsed. The water was choppy out in the bay, as the wind pushed through the inlet and swayed the trees...

Jim's eyes stayed fixed on the body in front of him; his face had become expressionless as his thoughts had taken him far adrift; Anna was fixed too on the body as she scratched Jim's back. Both were quiet for a while as they experienced the moment, but Jim began to fret and wonder about what to do now; what should be done, he worried; what did he have to do to, he questioned, in order to straighten out this crooked line. 'The time is out of joint,' he quoted in his mind. 'Oh, cursed spite, for ever I was borne to set it right!'

Anna patted Jim's back and said, Well, cowboy, I am really hungry now! I'm going inside to have some lunch, finally. Jim stood and looked on Anna as she hopped off of the bench. She buttoned her blouse, tucked it into her skirt and pulled the skirt back over her hips, straightening the stockings on her thighs a bit. Anna kissed Jim, realizing that he would need to be alone for a few minutes. You are incredible, she said in his ear, and she walked outside, disappearing behind the door of the boat house.

Jim turned back toward Mary's body and sat down; he stared at the now strange body which hung dead before him, the empty body which had housed his beloved Mary. 'The time is out of joint,' he thought, Shakespeare's voice in *Hamlet* was right, the time is out of joint. Jim turned and, pulling up his pants and tucking in his shirt, made steps for the door; he went outside and shut the door of the boat house. The sky was clear, but for a few large summer clouds on a rich blue background. The wind pushed through the clouds and the trees on land and played with the surface of the water. Jim walked down to the small strip of beach between the dock and the nearby trees. Out across the bay he could make out a part of Ono Island and the inlet beach. All of it sang to Jim in this early afternoon Sun, which poured down its rays at an eastward angle, signaling the first beginnings of the golden light to come. The water invited Jim into its deep blue flow; occasionally spraying the air with a touch of the sea as it reached for the sky above. Jim floated in a natural concert with the scene around him; his spirit was now one with the world and he felt at peace for a moment.

There was no worry, no pain and no negation in this moment, there was only the pure affirmation of nature within the positive spirit of the human being.

It is the body, he thought, which represents the joint of time, and is usually conjoined as a kind of continuous ligament with it, yet here, in this body, hanging in that boat house, there is a point of time which no longer belongs to any such continuity. It is not merely a crooked line, but also a broken one, a brutally ruptured, painfully shattered, line of time, Jim philosophized. The body normally expresses its own time, as well as its own space, and this agrees with Spinoza and Kant, but here is a body which presently expresses nothing. It neither takes up the matter around it nor stratifies the time within it; it lies cold and stiff, if expressing anything, it only expresses non-expression. It is a frozen moment; a moment which no longer pursues the next moment of the future, nor does it become pushed by its moment of the past. It is a still and immobile moment, frozen within time. In this, it arrests a privileged line of temporal development while also setting into motion another one outside of itself. A vibrant life has been squelched in the passage of a single instant, while all the lives which continue around it will be altered without the possibility of avoiding it.

How can I have the gall, Jim thought, to be remotely happy on this day? Should I not be a broken man; sent into a tailspin because of Mary's death? No! I refuse. Anna has taught me that, at least; it does good to no person involved for me to loose control, even though I do feel a tremendous pain and an irreplaceable loss. But what is it that I do feel? I feel decidedly caught; that is what it is like; I am caught and suspended within a moment, which is neither my own nor anyone else's, it is only Mary's; it is Mary's last moment, which succeeds in catching and somehow suspending me in between a past and a now altered future. It is a prison, that I feel to be inside, which locates me within a cell of temporality.

I remember walking into the spare room, which Mary used for a studio, above the garage in Mobile; I saw her then, not two years after we were married, slumped over her easel, motionless.

...Mary?, I wanted to...Jim's words had stopped there, he could not figure out why she seemed to be so gloomy, for there was no indication of it before. They had some lunch earlier; some casserole and baked chicken; Mary said she would go upstairs and do some work, since she was still brainstorming a couple of ideas for canvases to put into a show. Jim found that he could only stand quiet, staring at her, as she slowly looked up from the easel.

Jim, I'm empty, she said. I don't see anything here. She pointed her brush at the oversized canvas which dwarfed her.

I'm sorry, he returned with knitted brows.

You're sorry; don't be sorry; you have ideas constantly, and here I am, in front of a huge canvas with nothing to paint. She sat frozen as Jim looked on, her left hand raised with a brush to the canvas above her sloping head, looking downward, away from the six-foot high monolith. But what is this canvas?, she thought. It is so prominent before me, a gaping window onto nobody-knows-what; is stares back at me, it takes up the pristine northern light from the great portal and sits in judgment, filling the room with a maniacal laughter; it is laughter at me, at what a loss I am; I suck; I am not up to the task to put anything to this canvas; I cannot make it be silent; it screams at me as I weep amidst my torture.

No Jim, don't be sorry, she said, as she sat still and motionless. Just enjoy your ideas.

But what was that?, she thought. Why did I have to make him feel guilty just then? Why should I allow myself to hurt him so much, when he has done nothing wrong? Mary stood and walked over toward Jim. She stopped, quietly facing him, and looked into his eyes, into his piercing eyes. She threw her arms around him saying nothing...

I was left without a clue as to what was going through her head, Jim thought, standing on the short sandy shore. She was beating herself over the head for an idea, completely impatient for inspiration. The paintings she did manage to finish were well received, but that large canvas in particular still stands in the studio untouched. I'll never forget how she looked while seated at that canvas; that in itself was a kind of artwork for me; the artist with nothing to say, for Modernism has said it all; of course, I could not have mentioned this to her, that she represented all which was at grief with Modern Art; that it was a loss of focus based on the over-attempt at focus; that art should not be treated like a career, with overemphasis upon production, but should be treated like the inspiration it is. Contemporary artists rack themselves with a tremendous amount of guilt if there is no constant

production, always steering between the *Scylla* of
inactivity and the *Charabdis* of over-productivity
applied to a dry palette, when dependence upon the
inspiration alone would easily navigate an artist
between these two extremes. What I feel within this
tragedy is the loss of meaning which would have come
from watching Mary develop into the mature artist who
would have easily solved these problems.

Having finished her lunch now, Anna had also
solemnly removed Mary's stockings and heels, now
wearing the sandal heels she wore when she arrived at
the house. She crept up behind Jim and put her arms
tightly around him, but, not wanting to make him self-
conscious, stayed out of his sight.

You miss her, she said, you love her.

Yes, he said, as he suddenly felt more tears
welling up within his eyes. I miss her dreadfully, he
thought. Never again will she smile; never again will
she laugh...I have you, Anna, he forced himself to say,
clasping her hands with his as the tears he had fought
rolled down his face.

Behind them, a Police patrol car drew up behind
the other cars, to settle close to the front of the house.
The blowing of the wind had prevented Anna or Jim
from hearing the car pull up, but when Officer Frank
Mclain got out of the car and shut the door, a small
noise made it to them and Jim turned around to see in
the distance the tall man of the law studying them. His

young brow was contemplative, and it acted as a shield
for his piercing eyes; his brown hair was kept trimmed,
and his uniform was black and crisp. He performed a
small wave with his right hand, which served as a
signal of his readiness to deal with the situation, but it
also acknowledged to them an unobtrusive stance not
characteristic of the local Police. Jim looked at Anna,
finding himself speechless, unsure of what was
happening. Anna returned his look, feeling the need to
explain.

He's here because of me, she said, I called them
while I was inside and talked to this very man, I think;
he is very nice; I only thought that we needed to get
Mary's body taken care of.

Yes, yes of course, Jim said, quickly realizing
the selfishness of his actions during the day; he thought
about how he had been dragging his feet on this matter
in particular, for fear of being accused of her death; of
course, he thought, I wouldn't be accused of hanging
my wife; of course, we should get the body to a proper
place, I guess the place will be crawling with these cops
and news people soon. I suppose that this is an
unavoidable consequence now.

Anna rushed over to greet Officer Mclain,
feeling that he was to be treated like a guest; she shook
his hand politely while Jim watched on from the sandy
shore.

Thank you so much, officer, for being discreet,
she said, looking into his dark eyes. She wanted to let
him know how grateful she was for his avoidance of
the lights and sirens, so she used her good old
fashioned charm to do the trick.

It's no trouble, he returned, not able to avoid looking at Anna inquisitively, as he noticed the few small curls, the locks, of her hair which curled around to tickle her eyelashes and cheeks. Her bright, clear eyes, slightly green, allowed him to immediately fall and become enraptured for a moment, they let him completely forget the lovely young lady he had met recently and asked out to diner. He forgot about her jet black hair and her soft white skin, her southeastern Mediterranean countenance which had mesmerized him over a plate of beef and a glass of wine. Anna was therefore very striking to him, and, as she spoke to him about Jim and Mary Mercer, he could not help but watch her face and visually play with her skin, noting her tall figure in her silk and wool outfit, and then return his gaze back into her eyes.

Well, Miss..., he quickly said, in an effort to interrupt his own disturbing thoughts and to banish painful memories.

Anna Lipscomb, she said, nodding her head slightly, shifting her weight from one foot to another.

Miss Lipscomb.

Anna, she said familiarly.

Miss Lipscomb, he stood, slightly set off by her wile; I suppose I should get to work, so you and Mr. Mercer might get on with your day.

Yes, she said; well, the body; is Mary now only a 'body?', she thought; the body, she continued, is in this storage house over here; she added a wave of her hand as she began to walk over toward the boat house. Mclain followed her, naturally trying hard to focus upon his task at hand and put other concerns aside, even though he could not help but notice her legs and stride, the cut of her skirt, or the highlights in the long locks of her dark hair. He forced himself to look away as he stepped up to the door of the boat house, but Anna stopped short, for she had no wish to go inside again. She would not want to see the dead body again, which so loudly screamed out its pain.

Moving inside, Mclain, though keeping his hand on the doorknob, peered into the scene of the incident. Mary Mercer hung, suspended from a noose, her body and face pale and blue. Her eyes were open, frozen within a gaze which looks no longer; her blonde hair was unkempt; her body was naked. Mclain surveyed the surrounding area, but it revealed no clues. There was only a stool which was presumably kicked over by Mrs. Mercer. There was no sign of any kind of a struggle, and no sight of any type of clothing. He circled around behind the body, looking for an instant into the clear water in the boat bay. He thought he saw something, but perhaps not, finding himself drawn to looking back at the body, as if forced. Mclain came back around to face Mary, looking right into her blue eyes; they were still quite clear and appeared vibrant, indicative of unique tenderness to him. Mclain could not help himself; he painfully remembered the clear eyes of his own wife, as she lay dead on the morgue table, the night he had been called in to identify her.

They were those same eyes which had years ago allowed him to feel familiar and loved; the same eyes, he remembered, which years ago, gazed back into his, as he stood upon the altar with his beloved. He always remembered the same intensity of the eye, and, even as she left him, when she was not quite in tears, and as she walked out of the front door to their house, she looked back only briefly, and then disappeared. But why has that come back, once again, to haunt me, he thought, time and time again?

The horror which had run through him, strong and like a bolt of lightning, became very real for him just once more; the only difference was that now it was a perfect stranger who lay in an upright death before him; a vertical tomb which was a cessation of the absolute pain. It was the clarity of the eyes which had drawn him in, as he realized them again to be the same eyes. He could not escape the emotions now as he felt only the shock and the cut of seeing his wife lay on the table, poisoned by the pills, having only a disrupting effect on her face. He saw only the double image of his wife and Mrs. Mercer, both dead and looking at him with the same eyes; they stared at him without even seeing him, and he saw them even as he looked away. It was his wife who hung by the rafters in this boat house, and it was his wife who stared at him through her eyes now. Mclain, profoundly disturbed and on the edge of complete breakdown, quickly turned away from the body and leapt toward the door as he blocked his tears. He stepped outside, holding his fingers to his eyes, and found Anna waiting outside. He fought his pain and pulled himself together only long enough for the instant it took to speak to Anna.

The coroner and an ambulance should be here shortly, he said, nodding his head as his face became red, and his eyes watered with tears.

That's fine, she said, realizing the officer must

be experiencing more emotions internally than had met her eyes before. She even wondered if the officer somehow knew Mary, perhaps he knew her quite well?

Mclain looked out at Jim Mercer as he paced back and forth on the short beach. In that single moment Mclain fully knew what must have gone through Mr. Mercer's mind, if, like Miss Lipscomb had reported, he had found the body earlier today. He knew well the pain Mercer had been feeling, he knew about the shock and horror, not only of being face to face with death itself, but with the untimely death of the one person closest to him, the one person to whom his own life was pledged. In that very moment Mclain felt, without restraint, the infinite pain of his own long despair, combined with Mercer's, now formed into a limitless feeling of absolute grief.

An ambulance drew up behind all the other vehicles and pulled through, farther toward the boat house. The driver and his partner got out and came toward Mclain, both younger than he; the driver, who had sandy colored hair and wore a mustache, and the other, who had her black hair pulled into a single ponytail, both seemed to know Mclain, as they acknowledged his presence in a familiar way. Mclain returned the gesture, but found himself torn. He had wished to go over to Mercer and tell him, from the standpoint of being human, that he understood, that he could well feel the same pain Mercer was feeling.

How does it look, Mclain?, Mike Baxter said, interrupting Mclain's thoughts. Mike looked over at Anna and then at Mclain, and set out trying to make sense of what might be going on between them. It's not enough for him to chase Deb, he thought, he has to go and be the big man in front of this fine lookin' lady.

Inside here, Mike, he returned curtly. Mike decided not to make a scene, here, and stepped into the boat house.

Hi Frank, Deborah Phillippa said, with a curled mouth; haven't seen ya' around much, guess ya' been busy, huh? Her face seized him and she teased him with her black eyes, as she toyed with him using the draw of her countenance. But, sensing how upset Frank seemed to be, and noticing Anna, she wondered what was happening between he and this older, seductive woman. He's just trying to make me jealous, she thought; and he knew we would get this call, I told him I was working this shift.

Yeah, I've been layin' low, he said, with a snicker, trying hard, but in vain, to avoid those black Mediterranean eyes of hers which were so powerful to him. Thanks for coming in quietly, though, he added, these folks don't want a big fuss.

Well, Anna interjected, I'm only looking out for dear Jim. She picked up the tension between Officer Mclain and this young girl, and thought she would clarify things; but only just a bit. He doesn't want a lot of attention about this, she added, it's embarrassing enough without the whole neighborhood standing here asking questions, she said, with emphasis, as she looked at Deborah, noticing her soft skin and dark eyes. Mclain slipped and allowed his mouth to curl a little, amused by Miss Lipscomb's stealth approach.

No problem, Deborah said with a smile which masked her immature jealousy, ever raging as she threw back a glance at Anna and Mclain. She vehemently hated him right then; she hated Anna and she hated what this made her look like to them. Deborah took her glance away, though, and walked into the boat house after Mike. Mclain turned to Anna and led her a couple of steps away from the boat house toward Jim.

If you have any problems, Miss Lipscomb, or if Mr. Mercer has any concerns, I'll be available to help. I'm gonna go on now and let these guys take care of things; I hope you have a good afternoon. He walked off toward his patrol car as Anna looked on. Deborah came out of the boat house and went over to the ambulance, watching Frank. He got into the car and slowly backed out of the drive. She watched him leave as she opened the rear door of the ambulance, then turned herself away, pulling a stretcher out. She took the stretcher into the boat house without looking at Anna or Jim. Anna then turned toward the beach and looked on as Jim stood with his back to the scene, lurking on the shore.

Another car pulled up an Anna turned to see; it was the county coroner; she pulled the car up beside the ambulance and got out. She acknowledged Anna, then walked into the boat house as if she knew exactly where she was going. Anna watched for a moment as the boat house stood silent, masking what was going on inside, then she turned toward the dock, feeling somewhat lackadaisical, digging the heels into the sand as she walked toward it. Jim watched her walk to the dock and down its length to *Ideal*, thinking about how Anna seemed so simplified, in a way, to him. She doesn't seem to feel pain very deeply, or is it that she feels it even deeper than I can imagine? Maybe she does feel it deeper and therefore manages to deal with it in a more efficient way. She is so beautiful to me right now; pristine and even youthful. I'd like to go up there, kiss her, and tell her how I appreciate her being here; but those strangers are here and they would not understand the situation between us.

Just then Anna looked into the sky; she could see the airplane crossing between two puffy clouds as it turned back in the other direction, westward. It must be the same one as before, she thought, the advertising for the bar. Jim looked up as well, noting the craft, watching it glide closer to the earth on its way down along the far away beach. He then was reminded of his run on the sand earlier; I don't know what I was doing, he thought, chasing into the future? If I could race into the *One*, what sort of a future would the chase reveal for us all? What part of our past would it attempt to leave behind?

Anna stepped out of her shoes and onto the deck of *Ideal*, and only kicked around, passing the time, playing with the lines and rigging, and felt the wind blow her clothing against her skin. Jim watched her intently, as she returned the glance back at him, looking at his mussed hair, wrinkled clothes and bare feet. She wanted to be able to forget about this unfortunate tragedy; she wanted to go out for a sail on the ocean and take a nap down below with the water lapping at the hull. Jim watched Anna's movements against the backdrop of the sky, naturally lulled by her beauty, by the outline of her figure underneath her clothes. But, almost frustrated by a nagging sensation, he asked

himself, what is the *One*?, as he looked back at the
disappearing plane on the far horizon. Why does the
unity of things guard such secrets? Is it that a
Radamanthus is sitting within the confines of the *One*,
dispensing forever his stern judgments?, or is there
some type of being laughing at me, laughing at my
sheer folly, with eyes which are directed at nothing?

With that, though, the plane disappeared behind
the trees and Jim turned, first toward Anna, then to the
boat house, just as the coroner, Mike and Deborah were
rolling out Mary's body. Jim looked at the black bag
which contained Mary with horror and puzzlement.
Anna sensed his emotion as she watched on and
suddenly perked up. She scampered back onto the dock
and to its end, while Jim watched them put Mary's body
into the ambulance.

Jim's thoughts began to race; what secrets; what
hides in the...when was it; that moment, it was that
moment, then on the altar...knelt before all...the sight of
her blonde hair on the white satin, so gently flowing;
the chapel...that moment with warm light; was it a
round room with golden lights all around?, no, it was a
ring, twirling through the air catching reflections, I put
on her finger...they were there, everyone in white...and
she, in that moment her eyes, she looked at me, her
eyes gleaming said to me...she whispered to me in that
dress, she said I love you...she smiled nervous, my
pulse, as I put that ring on her finger...the lights around
us to happy; we stood on the altar with the wind
blowing our hair, the light shown down as she smiled at
me and her eyes were so clear shining on me as I loved
her down to my core...everyone smiling and wiping

tears, with the music flowing, the strings, the organ the infinite pipes, and she whispered the I love you with those eyes...everyone smiling and the tears rolling down and down, they rolled down and covered the floor as we stood on the altar...the water floated us as the waves white capped and the wind blew...but now the light fades, becomes blue...everyone cries and the white goes gray, dirty with the tears, and becomes black as we stand on the altar, but Mary stops smiling...she looks at me and weeps with those eyes...she rises and levitates before me, she floats down to the water and dies; she goes away; a watery grave, as the ring comes off her finger and falls into the water...she lies in the coffin, white and blonde in the black coffin...stiff and cold in the seething earth...the dirt falling on her clean face; the strings crackle and the pipes bend as the people weep and Mary dies...the tyranny...the tyranny of the future, as Mary goes away covered by the earth in the black coffin...blonde hair stained by the dirt as the ring lies in my hand.

Jim froze his thoughts, then felt an infinite pain. He turned toward Anna and screamed in terror; he fell to his knees and put his head down to the ground; he was wailing, weeping for his loss and horror. Anna ran to him; she knelt down and put her hand on his back as he cried, and as the coroner shut the door on the ambulance. Mike and Deborah looked on as Jim cried, then got into the ambulance. The coroner stepped closer to Jim and Anna, but motioned to Anna to come over. Anna got up and walked over to her.

It's a good thing you are here, young lady, the

woman said, as her silver hair sparkled with the late Sun behind it; he will need a friend for a while.

Yes, Anna said, looking into the woman's soothing blue eyes.

I just want to tell you, since I won't bother Mr. Mercer now, that there is no evidence of anything other than suicide here. I don't suspect anything foul, so the police will likely not disrupt the rest of your day. The body will, of course, be available for the morticians tomorrow. Now, I found this, she said with a pause; she showed Anna her open hand which contained a gold wedding band; this was in the boat slip, down in the water, guess Mclain must have missed it. Anna said nothing as she looked at the Coroner's face, then the ring in her fingers.

Here, I suppose he will want this later, she said, giving the ring to Anna.

I imagine he will, Anna said.

Have a good night, Miss Lipscomb.

Thank you, Anna said.

The coroner walked back to her car, got in, and back away from the house; the ambulance followed, down the drive and out of sight. Anna watched as the vehicles drew away, unable to think about any face now but Mary's. She was fighting the temptation to burst into tears, only because she felt that Jim was in need of her strength and ability to keep a cool head. Inwardly, though, she felt the tremendous loss of her dear friend, and could not help but let a teardrop roll down her cheek. Even in her stoic denial of her pain, Anna could not begin to avoid it, but at the same time would not allow herself to become a sniveling girl.

Anna turned to Jim, looked at the ring and put it into her skirt pocket, thinking she would give it him later. She walked over to him, paused, looking at the sky, then knelt down behind him. There was no way she could avoid it now, she thought, there was no sense in trying to; the pain of losing Mary hit her broadside and there was no way out of feeling the effect. She lay herself onto his back, hugging him, and turned her face away, as a few more tears streamed out of her eyes.

Jim pulled his head up out of his lap and ran his hand through his hair, then, leaning on Anna, got up onto his feet, and found himself looking on the outline of *Ideal*; he felt himself beginning to think of how nice it would be to go out on the boat again. He could not help it; the boat called to him to go and explore his emotion by floating, both on the air and on the water.

Let's go for a sail, Jim said, without a care as to how Anna might feel about this new direction.

That would be great, Anna returned, as she quickly remembered her earlier wish to go out on the boat anyway. She therefore found it a wonderful idea and thought it would be a great way to let go of the stress of the day.

They made their way from the sandy point to the dock, walked along its length, then stepped up to the boat. Anna left her shoes and stepped over the rail onto the deck while Jim, pausing only to make sure that he still had the spare keys to the engine in his pocket,

handed the keys to Anna and again handled the shore
power and dock lines. Anna, feeling her thirst, went
below and looked for something to drink, finding only a
little wine and some bottled water. Jim jumped into the
cockpit to turn on the diesel and tidied the last of the
lines as Anna decided that the leftover wine, which Jim
had opened earlier in the morning, would be an
excellent stimulus to relaxation. She poured the rest of
the wine into two glasses and then stepped out of the
companionway, balancing herself perfectly in the
yawing boat, even thought it had been a while.

Enjoy!, she said, holding out a glass for Jim.

Thank you, Jim returned, looking into her eyes
for just an instant, then back onto the horizon of the sea
out beyond the reach of the inlet. He steered the craft
under power for a couple of hundred yards, then
hoisted the main. The wind filled the airfoil and lulled
the boat to a faster speed. Jim killed the diesel and
unfurled the genoa, which pulled the boat even faster.

They rode silently aboard *Ideal* as it took them
far out away from the bay, then to the increasingly aqua
water of the bayou and inlet, then past the tall 182
bridge and out past the rock jetties. The boat sliced
through each rolling wave of the sea as it moved out
and away from the Alabama coastline. Once out far
enough, so that the coast was barely visible, Jim furled
and dropped the sails to let the boat drift. He stood and
took Anna's hand and led her to the foredeck, where
they stood and watched the now fading light of the day;
the first few moments of the golden hour were bathing
the scene with warm light. They stood silent as they
watched the light fall into its amber mood, draping the

sky with orange overtones, then falling to the water to reflect the heavens in the waves. Jim and Anna held each other tightly as they let their tension fall with the light, massaged by the gentle waves of the sea in late afternoon.

I've got something for you, Anna said, visualizing the ring inside her pocket.

What's that, Jim wondered.

The Coroner gave this to me, she said, as she pulled the ring out and held it up for Jim. This is probably as good a time as any to give it to you, she added. It was in the water.

Jim was surprised upon seeing the ring, and held out his hand as Anna placed it in his palm. He looked at it over and over, yet said nothing. Jim could hear the shutter clap against the wall of the Mobile house in his head. His thoughts took him back to the library as his mother stood before him holding her purse.

...Thomas wouldn't believe it, she said.

Why not?, Jim asked.

He would never have left this house, not for any reason, and here I am leaving it behind. But I think he would approve of the new owner. Elizabeth Mercer had never even begun to question the wisdom of leaving the house to Jim at the age of twenty-two, but he had proved himself trustworthy, and, besides, she thought, why should I care anymore? I have to let the past go and move on with things. Let Jimmy stay here if he wants to; he'll take care of the place as well as he is able.

The shutter clapped harder against the wall as

the wind picked up outside, spurred by an afternoon storm which was blowing through. Jim and his mother stood silent for a moment, listening to the noise, for it was doubtless the case, Elizabeth thought, that they were remembering the same event, all so long ago.

He never made it out there to fix the shutter, Jim said solemnly. That weekend never came for him, did it Mom?

No, it didn't. But that was a long time ago, Jimmy. There is only one thing you can do now.

What's that?, Jim pondered.

Get out there and fix that damn shutter!, she said, pointing her finger in his face for emphasis and allowing a smile to cross her mouth. Let it go, Jimmy, she added. Let it go...

Jim looked back into his hand at the reflection of the falling light in the gold band. He took the matching band off of his left hand and put them together, rolling them over each other, taking note of the play of reflection on their surfaces. Jim stepped away from Anna and threw the rings out, as hard as he could, into the sea. As the rings flew through the air, Jim remembered his thoughts upon seeing Mary in the body bag; he knew he was putting things to rest because he had envisioned the ring resting in water, and how eery it was that Mary had thrown the ring into the water, as well. Anna watched, in amazement, as the rings flew from his hand, to the sky above the Gulf and then into the blue water far away.

I've got to let it go, Jim said, turning to Anna for approval.

You have, she said, walking toward him. She

hugged him around the torso and repeated; you have let it go, Jim.

I have a feeling that I'm going to regret that!, Jim called out to the sky, already missing the wedding rings which had graced He and Mary's hands for five years. He began to race with guilt, fretting over the loss of the symbols of his marriage, but slowly calmed down as Anna petted his back. She soothed his spirit with her silence and he regained his composure.

I have to go out and fix the shutter, he mumbled.

What?, Anna asked, perplexed as to what he was talking about.

Nothing; there is just something important that I have to do now.

They turned away from the bow of *Ideal* and made their way down the deck to the companionway. Anna put the empty wine glasses into the sink and they went into the forward cabin.

Jim took off his shirt and Anna loosened her skirt belt as they climbed into the berth and began to touch each other. Jim kicked off his pants with his legs as he unbuttoned Anna's blouse. He kissed her chest as she slipped her shoulders out of the silver silk fabric and removed her skirt, sliding it down her legs. They made out for several minutes, rolling back and forth on the berth, then Jim slid his hands over Anna, placing kisses down the length of her body. They played for a few more moments and then slowed the pace, settling down into the berth. They allowed themselves to fall prey to their drowsiness and Jim tucked himself in behind Anna, burying his face into the back of her head as a smile of comfort curled on her lips. They said scarcely a word to each other in those minutes, only kissing each other briefly, then after a short time, they both managed to drift off into a nap. Several times, Jim twitched himself out of sleep and sat up in the berth. Each time he looked out of one of the small cabin windows to make sure that the boat was not near danger, then he settled back into a comfortable sleep with his arms around her.

Anna floated far above the green sea, lifted by the warm air of the day, as it rose toward the purple sky. She saw Jim and Mary standing on the orange sand below, and they were waving to her to come and meet them. She drifted down to the beach as the yellow stars twinkled in the dome of the sky above, and stood facing the two of her friends. But Mary began to fade away, and Anna ran to grab her, before she could completely disappear, but she was too late. She grabbed at Mary, but her arms only curved around to meet her own shoulders. Jim stood behind Anna as they watched Mary ascend to the heavens. Her spirit was bright and punctured the dome of the purple sky, becoming the brightest, newest star of the firmament. Anna felt peace when she dreamt about Mary, and felt comfort about Jim, now. Her dream then faded into other scenes, as she slept soundly in Jim's arms with the water lapping at the hull of *Ideal*.

Jim was running across the white, hot sand, chasing the Sun, which was setting in the distance. His strides became longer as he ran, which sped him faster and faster down the length of the beach. He could hear, though, someone calling to him from behind, and he turned to see who it was. He saw Mary, calling to him, begging him to stop running, to come back and stay with her, for she wanted to trap him again within the frozen moment of her time. Jim ran faster, refusing to be lured by her pain. He chased hard at the Sun as Mary chased him, but as he got closer to the setting Sun, she got closer to him, and at the moment where they all three met...Jim was startled awake by a creak in the hull of the boat. His forehead was sweaty and he felt a dry mouth, but he looked out of the small window and figured that they should be getting back to the beach house sometime soon.

During their nap, the boat had drifted in the water, turning around and around as it floated, finding no point of contact with anything other than the soft water of the Gulf of Mexico. It had come toward the shore and floated far to the West, across the white beach of Gulf Shores toward Fort Morgan. Jim awoke one last time from his nap and looked out the side windows to get some idea of where they were. He realized that they were in no danger, but figured that they would have a long sail back, if the wind didn't pick up markedly. He noticed Anna rousing herself from her nap and laid down on top of her, kissing her on the cheek.

Let's go for a swim, he said, trying to contain the very immediate excitement that he was feeling, for his nap seemed to clear his conscience of any questions of the correctness of his actions, and it served to rid his emotions of any last traces of hatred toward Mary.

Okay, she returned, pushing him off of her and to the side. I'll beat you out there!, she added and lit off through the salon to the companionway. Jim got up and took off after her, catching her at the steps, grabbing her body in a bear hug and kissing her cheek; she paused for a moment to enjoy the attention, but then elbowed him in his chest and scampered up the steps and out onto the deck. Jim could not catch her before she dove off over the rail into the blue water; Jim followed her into the unknown, feeling the cold rush of the water over his skin; he felt completely at the mercy of the elements for a few instants as he slowly came up to the surface of the water, seeing Anna nearby.

I love you, Jim said, letting the rush carry him along without thinking about his words first. I have always loved you, he added. I will never forget Mary, I loved her dearly and she will always have a special place inside, but I do love you, Anna, I know all of this must be weird, but this is how I feel.

Jim, she said, allowing herself be serious for Jim's sake, but not insincere; I love you, too, with everything I have; I have loved you since we first became involved. I have never felt this way before, it kind of snuck up on me. The three of us had something together, but now it is different, and we are doing just what we should do. We can still mourn her, love each other, and go on.

Her words rang in Jim's ears; they allowed him to be completely at ease with the world, at ease with himself. They swam toward each other and hugged in the water for several minutes.

I guess we should be on our way back, he said reluctantly, it could take a while.

Let's go back and relax, for Pete's sake, she

added.   We could watch TV or a movie, or do
something mindless.   Jim laughed with a sincerity he
had not known lately.   How much emotion had he been
through today!, he thought.   It would feel good to at
least try to relax.

They climbed back on board the boat and Jim
hoisted sail; no one was within immediate sight, but
Anna retrieved their clothes from below and brought
them on deck.   Jim stepped into his khaki pants and
Anna slipped her black skirt over her hips, Jim put on
his shirt and Anna her blouse, and they tucked their
tails inside in an effort to look somewhat presentable, if
anyone were at the house when they returned.   They felt
the need to say little on the way back, feeling each
other's ease and comfort, as well as enjoying the sail.

They made their course eastward, across the
coast line, back to the inlet, tired and very hungry.   The
wind had picked up slightly in the early evening sky,
allowing them to make hull speed for much of the time,
as *Ideal* pointed high on the southeasterly wind.   The
boat made it to the jetties and in through the inlet, under
the bridge and toward Sandy Point at Orange Beach.
Jim furled the head sail and put the weather cover on
the main, while Anna went below, cleaned up the galley
and got the garbage together to take inside.   She balled
everything up to tote it all under her arm, and climbed
out onto the deck.   Once back to the dock, Jim took a
few minutes to moor the boat snugly, thinking he would
not be able to come out to sail for some time, until after
the funeral.

We should go inside and get cleaned up before
everybody wants to come over, Jim said, as he finished

cleating the last of the lines, while Anna started to put the companionway hatch down, locking it.

Yeah, I feel pretty dirty from the seawater, as she climbed over the rail and onto the dock, and the sweat, she added, snickering and nudging Jim. He smiled at her, almost blushing.

They made their way toward the front door of the house; Jim looked out intermittently at the water as he walked, noting the trees as they swayed, and the clouds as they glided by in the evening sky. His mind was tired and needed to rest; he could have a drink, perhaps, and a bath would be good; he wanted to spend a little time coasting along without unnecessary energy; a time to work out for himself what sense this all could make, and allow Mary to become a meaningful experience for him, rather than a nightmare to fear.

Just as Proust had said, Jim thought, I needed to make Mary into a divinity within my consciousness, within my web of meaning; I needed to find the affirmation of life within Mary's personality, work and life, rather than be buried within her lie, within her cloaking of the truth of her existence. He paused for an instant at the door and continued to gaze out at the water, releasing his anger and pain over Mary as best he could, fully realizing that this would be a long process of discovery, an apprenticeship which would slowly reveal the meaning and impact of his life with Mary.

Anna disappeared into the house and Jim turned toward the front door again and went in. He then went to the wet bar adjoining the kitchen and mixed some gin from the bottle in the cabinet below and some tonic from the small refrigerator, while Anna dropped the garbage from the boat into the can under the sink in the kitchen. As he sipped on the drink he wandered around the house, and Anna went upstairs. He went over to the stereo across the den and put on some music, allowing whatever was already on to play; it was something from a Chopin collection; some etude, he thought, I can't place it right now, I'm so tired; it was in *Five Easy Pieces*, he remembered, but he began to wander around the room, listening, floating. He made his way to the parlor and sat slumped in the high back chair for a while, sipping his gin and listening to Chopin. The direction became clear to him as he floated; the process of discovery had begun even today, as he began to reflect on the day. Mary would never be forgotten, but made into a positive part of his personality, he thought. I do miss her, though, he lamented, as the etude came to an end.

Jim got up onto his feet and made his way to the foyer and stepped up the stairs while the next selection of piano music began; he slowly crawled up to the bedroom as the music faded from his ears, but he did not see Anna anywhere. A breeze was coming through the open doors into the bedroom as the light was beginning to fade in the evening sky.

Jim stepped into the bathroom and found Anna fully relaxed in a drawn bath, nearly asleep, surrounded by a few lit candles. Jim sat down in the wicker chair near the glass doors. I am exhausted, he thought; how far I have traveled today! The memories and emotions fly at me, but what will they mean for me? They are all signs and embers, standing for some hidden meaning, which I shall have to come upon slowly. His thoughts turned toward the family members, so distant from his mind all day. I suppose I must call Mary's father in Point Clear, and my mother in Fairhope, he thought; but how does one go about saying such a thing? How should I break such earth shattering news to them? How can I save them from the devastation which, I suppose is inevitable? I fear they will blame me for Mary's suicide, and will they not want to come right over here and talk about it all night, when I have given myself so much time to make sense of it? I suppose I have been selfish with the day, when I should have called them hours ago. Jim thought to call out to Anna, but realized that she would not want to be disturbed. I might have to go back to Mobile, he thought, for a day or two, as he walked over to the bed and picked up the phone, I'll have to hold a wake and manage the funeral along with Mary's father.

Anna felt completely relaxed and allowed her stress to be released, sinking her head down into the soapy water, then coming back up to rest her head on the edge of the tub. The light from the candles dripped warm light onto her skin and she fell into a nap, bathed in the soft glow.

Jim thought to himself, I have to deal with all of these...people...and arrangements, as he began to dial the number which would ring Mary's father, realizing it was going to be a long night of talking to many people and fielding their understandably hysterical reactions, it would happen like a rippled wave moving out in all directions from the scene of Mary's act; all of those loved ones will go through the arresting effect of Mary's last breath, just as he had; they will suffer the horror of her sudden suicide, and ask themselves why, just as he had. He paused from dialing and put the receiver back down onto the hook to take another moment to himself, just one more instant of study before being pulled out into that wave with them.

Jim's eyes fixed onto the reflections of light in the melting ice cubes, the liquid light within the gin and the prism of light from the glass in his hand; he looked around the room, taking in the warm yellow-pink glow, made from the incandescent lamps bouncing their photons off of the pastel colored walls; he looked outside, past the balcony at the now faded blue firmament of the day, a stage of blue so deep as to almost disappear within its eminent fall into the black sky of the encroaching night. Jim's soul glided out of the room, past the balcony doors with their wisping curtains, out to the tops of the trees, then out over them to the sky above Perdido Bay, the sky which became one with the southerly breeze and last light of the Sun which had already dipped below the horizon. Jim reached with his soul, with his imagination, to be a star within that deep firmament, to be one with the stars of the heavens as he glided over the whole of the earth. Jim heard the voices of all those who were a part of his life, taking in their soft clamor, their love and meaning; he saw their faces, lit by the last possible glow of the day, suspended above the sea there with him. There with him, floated Mary's father and his mother; he saw his father, then Anna, and then he could fix upon Mary's face, smiling at him with a finality and serenity he had not seen for some time. He brought them all into focus and found them to be a comfort to his troubled soul.

The ruptured lines of time; the shattered fragments of emotion; all of them came back together for Jim. The magnetizing effect of his soul served to draw them all up into a continuous identity, into a complete being, one being which freely contained the happy memories of his life and the disturbing pain of Mary's disillusionment and suicide; the affirmative part of his life and passion as well as the troubling questions of his marriage. Jim floated out on the ether clouds of the nebulous region of his mind and found the strength to put all of the broken pieces back together; to mend all of the torn seams of his mental flesh which had produced so much shattered emotion today.

This was not an end to the pain or to anything else, he thought, but a beginning to the process of making things fit back within one another, which would come during the future restructuring of his mental life. This future was now his own again and he was released from the talons of the present, of Mary's present, and his father's present, which had kept them securely imprisoned, and which had kept him equally trapped within its grasp. But, he asked himself, was it all ever a part of his task? Was this to be made a part of his apprenticeship; to be frozen within the frame of Mary's death; to lie within the moment? This was no question which he could have easily answered or which could have been adequately stated at this point, but it was a question which would certainly occupy the bulk of his time to come.

Anna squirmed around in the bathtub as she slowly came up from her sleep, caressing her legs and arms with the bubbly water. Jim's thoughts turned back toward the house from far above, but not yet back into it, as he allowed himself to see the scene around his body; the glowing room, Anna in the bath with the candles dancing warm light about her; the beach house, standing on the sandy point, with the boat house and *Ideal* nearby; the lapping water of the bay. Jim's eyes slowly came back toward the room; down from the heavens, down to the bay, across the treetops and into the bedroom past the glass doors and curtains, stirred by the gentle breeze. He made himself pick up the phone again, and, dialing Mr. Louis' number, thought about how distanced from, and at the same time connected to, the process, which he knew he had to begin.

Publishing Within the Moment
a retrospective

✳

Because I spent so much of my youth and mind discovering myself and the world, working so hard, learning to express myself through early books, the next most important thing to me after the expression was to remain independent. Unlike most other writers of the day, I did not want to spend years submitting my work to agents and editors, hoping to be the one-in-a-million selected through potential whim, only to suffer being told what I should have written or could write in future, what was selling that year. In ages past, the ages of which I most studied, it wasn't mere marketing that drove the writing, production, and selling of books, but the power of one's *ideas*. If a book was written, and if the author wanted it to be published, it usually was - perhaps with some exceptions, but very few books went unpublished.

"Perhaps the triangle of enigmatic, erudite characters, whose decadence and intelligence worked to create such a disturbing story, expressed something more honest and complicated, more real if you will, than I might have accomplished in another form."

By the 1990s, the business of publishing had

fully consumed the literary merit writing once held. Books had become products, something to be sold, rather than springboards for "risky" and unmarketable ideas. Selling dominated most writing, less concerned with honest expression, something which might not sell. In such a dystopian environment, it was considered strange and socially scary for a writer to publish their own work, because there was no way they could compete in the book business, and worse, because such an author could not be controlled by the gatekeepers. Somehow, writing was forgotten, a quaint throwback to a time when people actively read and sought out new ideas.

> "I was fascinated by the fact that anyone could set up their own publishing company, format the text, design the cover, and have it printed or produced for download. That they could do it and no one could stop them was most energizing, and offered...a sense of what publishing was supposed to be"

Despite this grim picture, I set out to debut with my sixth book in the spirit of the old small presses, like Whitman, Woolf, virtually all writers before big media. It was the same spirit with which many musicians and filmmakers have slowly undercut the editorial power of record labels and film studios, who are part of the same companies who own the big publishers. Although I had a lot to learn, I was fascinated by the fact that anyone could set up their own publishing company, format the text, design the cover, and have it printed or produced for download. That they could do it and no one could stop them was most energizing, and offered a hint of danger, a sense of what publishing was supposed to be - the distribution of ideas allowing us to think. Although, I would be willing to accept the spoils of potential sales, my chief concern was for the work to *exist*.

Had I been concerned with the petty business of publishing, with merely pushing product, I would not have written such a challenging and dense, yet cathartic and rewarding novella, which, like Poetry, would be very hard to "sell". Had I been worried about what agents and editors thought as the gatekeepers between writers and readers, I would not have purposely woven so many separate genres together, nor would I have purposely broken so many conventions of spelling, punctuation and compressed dramatic action. Had I been concerned with maximum sales, I would not have formed rimric press, nor worked as hard as I did to get the small exposure I did receive for the book. rimric became one of the first small publishers listed in a newly extended Barnes & Noble collection, and I embarked on a regional book tour.

That there was a welcoming and positive reaction from real readers to this novella was very rewarding. Perhaps the triangle of enigmatic, erudite characters, whose decadence and intelligence worked to create such a disturbing story, expressed something more honest and complicated, more real if you will, than I might have accomplished in another form. The story is woven from elements of so-called literary, romantic, and decidedly erotic fiction, but also with purple prose, academic writing and prose poetry. The styles within the book, as they are likely present within our own lives, offer a jumble, a kaleidoscope of words, thoughts, memories, experiences.

Of course, I learned many lessons - those of a writer working in a handwritten, free-writing mode of expression, and those of a small publisher working under an old, yet new, model. I wouldn't change any of it now, and I offer this edition of *To Lie Within the Moment* in a new design with my heartfelt thanks to all who helped me learn those lessons along the way. I'd set out to make an honest expression through fiction of my own romantic loss, my own intellectual search, to capture and reveal the moment with integrity. I'm humbly pleased it was a success and led to the books which followed.

M.R.M. Parrott
Chicago, June 2008

Notes on the Text and Cover Art

*

The 2008 edition had minor formatting changes to the original 1998 text. In the 2025 edition, extensive yet still minor edits have been made for clarity, among other minor changes. More of the conceptual and foreign language terms have been italicized for emphasis. Intentional spelling choices (and counter-choices given my eclectic styles) have been left intact among minor updates, and ellipses have been added to indicate abrupt scene changes more clearly.

The punctuation remains, inspired by Virginia Woolf - single quotes for dialogue, run-on and broken sentences, long paragraphs, semi-colons as emotional breaks. These were also intentional in my companion Philosophy book, *The Empiricism of Subjectivity*. For one example of many, Anna makes a terrible discovery:

> Why did you do this!, she yelled at Mary, I've been waiting around and you were hanging out here! You bitch!, Anna screamed, you stupid bitch!, why did you do it!?; we were supposed to have lunch, she said, more quietly, and with a rush of tears.

We can compare with this version:

> "Why did you do this?" Anna yelled at Mary. "I've been waiting around and you were hanging out here! You bitch!" Anna now screamed. "You stupid bitch! Why did you do it? We were supposed to have lunch," she added more quietly with a rush of tears.

Anna has just had an awful shock. The first version captures the frenetic pace, the mental changes of direction, the intensity of the words and emotions. The second version is standardized and boring, losing the rhythm and energy of the first with too much punctuation and separation. This is why *To Lie Within the Moment* has the style it has.

Indeed, the second style is used for the *Timeless* novels because I wanted standard language to offset the extremely complex plot and large cast of characters. It was necessary in order to keep track of exactly who is saying what to whom. In *Moment*, however, as well as *Subjectivity*, the deeper meaning and emotion of how it all comes together makes the book richly complex to me. This is why I used language as a fractured set of reflections strung together, "the ruptured lines of time" Jim feels. Scenes and voices abruptly change, the language moves from calm to furious and back again, and the reader is invited to flow from the thoughts of one character and their related omniscience to another.

For the new cover, the 2008 layout has been recreated and redesigned to fit the full-wrap printed paperback cover in addition to the ebook screen layout. The cover art was captured in 1994 near *B.J.'s Seafood* (one of the real yet erstwhile locations in the book). The out-of-print 1998 hardback cover art has also been added to the new cover for historical reference.

M.R.M. Parrott
Charleston, June 2025

M.R.M. Parrott's books include the novel trilogy, *Timeless*, travelogue *Driving Home*, Philosophy and Science series *Dynamism*, stage play *Ctrl-V*, with monographs in Philosophy, and chapbooks of Poetry and short stories.

mrmparrott.com

rimric press